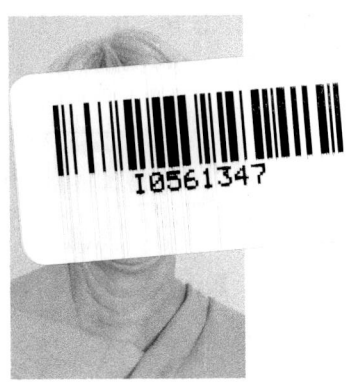

Karen grew up in a small country town in north-eastern Victoria, Australia. She spent her childhood riding horses through beautiful scenery of eucalypts, lakes, and snow-capped mountains and her love of landscape deeply affects her writing. She worked in a range of educational settings and holds a Ph.D. and M.Ed. (Hons) in the areas of fantasy. She is particularly interested in the power of the hero's inner journey which she explores through Deep Fantasy. Karen has travelled extensively overseas but enjoys nothing more than camping in the Australian Outback. She lives in Melbourne and now writes full-time. You can find out more about Karen and her books on her website.

Connect with K. S. Nikakis

Amazon: https://www.amazon.com/author/ksnikakis
Twitter: https://twitter.com/KSNikakis
Facebook: www.facebook.com/ksnikakis
Goodreads: www.goodreads.com
Website: www.ksnikakis.com
Email: author@ksnikakis.com

WORKS BY K S NIKAKIS

Non Fiction

Journey: Seeking the Sacred, Spirit and Soul in the
Australian Wilderness

Fantasy Novels
Series

Angel Caste series:
Angel Blood
Angel Breath
Angel Bone
Angel Bound
Angel Blessed
Angel Caste – Complete 5 Book Series

The Kira Chronicles trilogy:*
The Whisper of Leaves
The Song of the Silvercades
The Cry of the Marwing
remnant hard copies only

The Kira Chronicles series:
The Whisper of Leaves
The Silence of Stone
The Secrets of Stars
The Thunder of Hoofs
The Crying of Birds
The Music of Home
The Kira Chronicles – Complete 6 Book Series

Fantasy Novels

The Emerald Serpent
Heart Hunter
The Third Moon
Messenger
I Heard the Wolf Call My Name – *Finalist - Best YA Novel*
Aurealis Awards, 2019

Fantasy Short Stories

The Gift
The Tale of Prince Anura
Dragon Sprite
Glass-Heart – *Finalist –*
Best YA Short Story Aurealis Awards, 2019

Angel Caste

Book 2 Angel Breath

K.S.Nikakis

Angel Caste – Book 2 Angel Breath

First published by SOV CONSULTING LLC - SOV Media Australia 2017 Amazon: www.amazon.com.au

Publisher: SOV CONSULTING LLC - SOV Media Melbourne, Australia.

Cover by AS Nikakis: http://asnikakis.com
Shutterstock.com/ schankz
DaFont.com/Abdullah Alkhafaji – Ghost Theory 2

National Library of Australia
Cataloguing-in-Publication entry:
Nikakis, Karen Simpson
The Angel Caste series – Book 2 Angel Breath
ISBN 978-0-6489797-5-3

Learn more about KS Nikakis and her deep fantasy books at: http://www.ksnikakis.com

For the Terang Gang – Sue and Rick Broadway

Glossary of the Rynth

ANGEL CASTE

Crystal Fold
Principae (*prin-sip-ay*)
Nearest to ultimate transcendence. Manifest as aqua light, with white wings and group consciousness. The Principae transcend Crystal Fold to the Great Beyond.

Ezam Fold
Archae (*ar-kay*)
Five levels: angels ascend from Quin-archae through Quar-archae, Tri-archae, Du-archae, Prime-archae up to Archae. The Archae transcend Ezam Fold to Crystal Fold to become Principae, then transcend to the Great Beyond.

Members of the Archae
Archae Kald
Archae Dejon (*day-jon*)

Members of Prime-archae
Prime-archae Mirek
Prime- archae Serith

Dane
Lowest in the hierarchy and newest angels to Ezam. Ascend from Dane to Quin-archae, and then through the hierarchy to Archae to eventually transcend to Crystal Fold as Principae, and then to the Great Beyond.

Members of Dane
Thrisdane
Kydane (*kie-dane*)
Ashdane

DAIMON CASTE

Reside in any fold where angel caste has joined with other castes and produced offspring. The term is also used for those who have *any* angel caste heritage.

Moonsun Fold
Viv Wright

HUMAN CASTE

Moonsun Fold
Members of Human Caste
Lettie Wright – Viv's mother
Jimmy (Ronald James) Wright – Lettie's husband
Rim (Rimmon) – gang leader

Wheel Fold
Scharii – travelling musicians (*shar-ree*)

Members of the Scharii
Tarchen en-Scharii (*tar-chen*)
Darch en-Scharii

About Wheel Fold: The eight sectors or Vales of Wheel Fold are: Eshavale, Ascavale, Warinavale, Genessavale, Beshavale, Terissavale, Sonoravale and Morvavale. These run north-south or cloudwise-starwise from the hub/peak:Astraal. The lake and city are also called Astraal.

Directions
Cloudwise -north
Starwise- south
Nightwise – west
Sunwise – east

Time Divisions
Zadicans (years) are divided by zadics of 45 days that include a period of recalibration in between (Vorash). Zadics are marked by constellations which appear and disappear in the night sky. Each has a particular meaning. The zadics are: Pool, Cascade, Fire, Ice, Lirium, Glimwing, Cadestone and Horse. Other brief zadics (Call Zadics), are meaningful to individuals and indicate the individual should visit the sacred city.

Each Vale has countless smaller valleys or vals. Each Vale has a main river eg Eshavale - Eshacade; Ascavale - Ascacade etc. Settlements near the river take their name from the river eg Esh-embrin; Esh-accom. The tributaries flowing from the vals are rills. Smaller settlements (setts) take their name from the rills eg Scinta-ril. Inhabitants of these sets are identified by their sett: Ataghan en-Scinta-ril; Sehereden en-Scinta-ril.

Eshavale – sector of Wheel Fold

Members of the Eshadi
Ataghan en-Scinta-ril – Syld, band leader, lein to Sehereden (*ata-gan*)
Sehereden en-Scinta-ril – lein to Ataghan, member of Ataghan's band (*se-hera-den*)
'Poss' – a lost child found by Viv

Brithergen – member of Ataghan's band
Jethren – member of Ataghan's band
Anthran – member of Ataghan's band
Daran – member of Ataghan's band
Sandagh – member of Ataghan's band (*san-da*)
Inaghan – member of Ataghan's band (*in-a-gan*)

Eshadi Sylds (acknowledged leaders)
Ataghan en-Scinta-ril
Darthen en-Within-ril
Mathian en-Fessen-ril
Garath en-Moss-ril
Kurnen en-Vara-ril

LEFER CASTE

Wheel Fold
Lefer Caste are bird/bat-like beings with human caste-like intelligence

Members of Lefer Caste
Roaith en-Leferen – blue crest (*ro-aith*)
Garian en-Leferen – red crest – alpha of the Rookery

BEASTMAN CASTE

Beastman Fold
Beastmen are puma-human mix creatures with human caste-like intelligence

IDIOMATIC EXPRESSIONS COMMON IN AUSTRALIA

Viv is Australian and uses a range of idiomatic expressions.

Keep tabs on – check on; monitor
Didn't wash/did wash – didn't/did sound true; wasn't/was acceptable
On the line – to take a risk/be at risk
Knocked-up – made pregnant; being pregnant
Get out of jail free card – from a board game where a special card grants the player advantages
Second chance draw – another ticket is picked out from the losing tickets in a lottery
Sticks the boots in – attacks physically or verbally
Dodged the honesty bullet – to 'dodge a bullet' is to escape something bad
Brownie points – points awarded by doing good deeds that will eventually grant a reward (from the junior group in the Girl Guides movement)
Take the cake – win the prize

Angel Caste Book 2
Angel Breath

Chapter 1

The rift's swirling colours looked the same as the last rift's but Viv had no idea if that were a good sign given she had ended up with the cat creature last time. Again there was no sense of movement, just the glimpse of a new fold at the end of the tunnel. It rushed towards her with terrifying speed and then she was tossed out into sand. For once she managed to keep her feet. Bloody typical, she thought, given the sand made a nice soft bed to land on.

There was no shortage of it either. Dunes stretched away in every direction like an immense bowl of whipped cream. Viv slowly turned, hoping *not* to see anything that resembled a cat creature and saw nothing at all. No palm fronds waved above the dunes, no birds arced across the sky, no animal left its prints. It was silent too, as if she had dropped into the middle of nowhere.

Emptiness was better than savage cat creatures, she reminded herself, and hugged herself as she forced visions of Thris's ravaged body into the cage with the other rats of memory. She took a moment to steady then set off up the nearest dune. It was a steep climb and the view from the top was of more sand which, as it turned out, was the view from the top of the second, third, fourth and fifth dunes after which she gave up counting.

She toiled on and as time passed, the mild air grew neither warmer nor cooler. TV docos suggested that deserts boiled by day and froze by night, but this one seemed as kindly as Ezam perhaps because, like Ezam, it had no sun.

Nothing alarming happened, in fact, nothing happened at all, including coming across a rift but finding a rift out was only one of her problems. Knowing where it went, staying alive in a new fold where witch-burning might be a sport, finding her mother . . .

Maybe Thris had planned to teach her more about rift travel before they left Ezam but she had not given him the chance. Forcing their departure might not have been one of her smarter ideas, she conceded, as she trudged to the top of yet another dune.

The view was the same and she swore, dropped the pack and flopped down beside it, sick of the monotonous landscape. She had read somewhere that if you were right-handed, you took slightly longer steps with your right foot so that, over time, you walked in circles. Great! She was going to spend her very long-life going around and around on this endless, bloody beach except to do a *decent* reconnoiter, all she had to do was fly!

Simpler said than done, she thought, as she recalled her disastrous first attempt, although this time she did not have to throw herself off a mountain. In fact, the empty sands provided an ideal place to learn to fly *properly*. It might even be fun given there was no one around like Ky to ogle her breasts.

Viv took off her shirt and camisole and stuffed them in the pack, then shortened the pack's straps and fastened around her waist. The pack was not heavy but it was awkward and she would have left it on the sand had she been confident she could return to it.

She tensed as she visualised wings but there was less pain this time and quickly over with. Angels did not seem to suffer *any* pain so maybe her human part caused it *or* her inexperience. She hoped it was the latter. She imagined spreading her wings and felt them flex, but the fold's even light threw no shadows and she brought them forward over her shoulders to admire them.

Her feathers were just as lustrous as she recalled and she caressed them in delight. Viv had owned few pretty things in her life and after her mother had gone, Jimmy Wright had smashed or hocked them but no one could steal her wings.

She straightened them again, thrilled by her control and considered how best to beat them. She did not want to zoom off like a rocket or crash land and break something. She had no idea whether angels could bed broken wings or repair them inside their bodies and was terrified of the possibility of a broken wing hanging from her shoulder, images of witch-burnings never far away.

She considered how Thris had beaten his wings at Haven and felt her feathers stroke her back. Pulses of sweetly scented air swirled about her and she felt a glorious sense of joy. She stilled her wings, discarded the pack, and took off the rest of her clothes. She might be only half an angel but with her wings and exquisite scent, she felt a hell of a lot more.

She quickened her wingbeats and gasped as she felt herself lift, then visualised flying forward, picked up speed, managed to slow, tilted to the right and flew in a large circle. She kept close to the ground and monitored how the angle of her body changed according to her speed. She practised slowing and speeding up and, after a while, was confident enough to enlarge the circle and fly higher. It gave her a better view of the fold and told her the dunes stretched to the horizon in every direction.

'How can there be a whole world made of sand?' she muttered then recalled the immense deserts of home. But this was not Australia or anywhere else she knew of and there might be *no way out*. Her wings lost their rhythm and she pitched forwards before she managed to steady. Thris said if there were a rift in, there was a rift out *if* you could find it. She gripped the feather at her neck but one way or another, Thris was gone. Get used to it, Viv. You are on your own.

She landed in a series of awkward drops like a falling spider, visualised bedding her wings and grinned as she wriggled her wingless back. She might be slow and clumsy but she could unbed her wings, fly, and bed them again. Not bad considering she was like an adult baby learning to walk.

Viv dressed and resumed her trek but it was so tedious she took to the air again, taking the pack with her. She flew naked, rested, and flew again, and as she became stronger and more confident, flew higher and faster. The sweep of air over her breasts and belly gave her the freedom she had long craved. There were no hard eyes upon her and no hard hands and, in the end, there was no fear. Laughing with delight, she flew on and on.

Chapter 2

Ky and Ash hurtled through the rifts, cradling Thris between them. Ash's speed and accuracy were so unerring Ky relinquished his will to the blue angel and might have believed himself in a human caste dream except for Thris's ravaged body.

Sand Fold, Moth Fold, and Hearth Fold passed in a blur and then they burst into Crystal Fold, fell to their knees, and bowed their heads. A wind whipped their hair about their faces and when it stilled, Thris had gone.

Ky toppled sideways onto the silvery grass and sobbed and then smelled Ash's sweetness as the blue angel's wing enclosed him in love and protection. 'How can Thris survive this?' he whispered. 'How can he live?'

'There is no death,' said Ash gently, 'just a passing on.'

'He would be dead to *us*, lost to *us*,' said Ky taking a ragged breath. 'I was his Shadow. I was supposed to protect him.'

'Angels have free will. He chose to do as he did.'

'It was because of *her*,' said Ky thickly, managing to sit. 'Because of the shekinah. Prime-archae Serith was right to seek her destruction. If he had succeeded—'

'He would be guilty of murder,' said Ash, 'and would have betrayed all the Host holds most dear. Thris chose this, Ky.'

'No!'

Ash rose and offered Ky his hand. 'Come.'

'We should wait,' said Ky not moving.

'Your wounds must be seen to. The Principae will call us when it is time to return.'

10

Ky took his hand and struggled upright. '*If* there is a time to return,' he said bitterly and then his eyes fastened on Ash's wings. 'You have white plumage,' he gasped.'

'Yes.'

'But . . . how is it possible?'

'Many things occurred in your absence, Ky, but I will not speak of them here.' They gripped hands and stepped into a rift but it was not until they neared Haven that Ash described his vision in the Blue Helixai.

'However it came about, I am thankful you saw the attack,' said Ky. 'I could not have brought Thris back alone. And I must still retrieve the shekinah.'

'You must recover first,' said Ash, 'and report to Archae Dejon. And I must speak with Prime-archae Mirek.'

'You have a mentor?' asked Ky in surprise.

Ash shook his head and smiled. 'A friend perhaps.'

Ash was grateful Prime-archae Mirek listened to his tale without interruption for its retelling was so distressing he had trouble getting to the end. 'When you fled the Larimar Stele, I feared the worse,' said Mirek, 'and so it has turned out to be. Do you believe the Principae will heal Thrisdane?'

Ash's shoulders slumped. 'They know he attacked the shekinah.'

'*And* defended her and the cost of that defence,' said Mirek and glanced at the surrounding shelves. 'There is much in these scrolls that suggest the paths to ascension are far less clear than many angels believe. Achieving a type of truth is not the same as failing to err, Ashdane, and I am starting to wonder whether a pure heart might count for more than both those things.'

As Ash winged away, he knew the Prime-archae had sought to comfort him but the Prime-archae's words haunted him instead. Having been tempted by the shekinah, he knew his own heart was far from pure and Ky's desire for the shekinah had turned to antagonism, an even more damaging emotion.

The Blue Helixai glowed against the umber sky and its beauty eased Ash's worries even before he reached his favorite cavern. He went swiftly along the tunnel to where a pool would be and knelt to wash away Thris's blood. His reflection was haloed with stars, an illusion he knew, that was created by the crystals in the stone. He closed his eyes as he washed, his thoughts on his injured friend and did not see the halo remain unchanged, despite the water's ripple and splash.

He went on, barely aware of his body coming into alignment or of the tunnels rearranging themselves to allow him passage. He rarely harmonised anymore for the mountain gifted him a symmetry more perfect than any he achieved on his own.

The lyre was in its usual place on the slab but Ash was too weary to play. He lay down beside it, expecting the core's wind-music to soothe him but his head filled with strange and disturbing images: storming sand; an angel plunging wingless from a cliff; feathers drifting down to a river's dark bed. The horror was so great he wept and it was his tears that finally brought him the peace he craved.

Archae Dejon drained his goblet of ambrosia in a single gulp as he considered Kydane's news. He had ordered Kydane to speak to no one and sent him to Haven to rest but there was another witness to Thrisdane's catastrophic failure and that was Ashdane. Dejon guessed Ashdane had already spoken to Prime-archae Mirek, for the two were in accord but even so, the only angels who knew of Thrisdane's likely demise were a Prime-archae and two lowly Dane.

Dejon's tongue flicked along his lips as he considered the implications. Mirek had already taken his concerns about Ashdane's *dreams* to Kald and, given Kald's reaction, would be reluctant to repeat the experience. Kald might even remain ignorant of the events until Thrisdane was well enough to tell Kald himself *if* he ever were *or* until Dejon informed him. But Dejon felt no triumph at his new-found power. Kydane's revelation the shekinah was winged changed everything.

His hand went to the jug of ambrosia but he stopped himself and wandered about his rooms instead. Given what had happened, Prime-archae Serith's rantings seemed almost prophetic. Thrisdane was the strongest, the most sensitive to rifts, the most skilled in transiting, and the most self-disciplined of the Dane and if Kald had not claimed him, Dejon certainly would have, and yet Thrisdane had failed cataclysmically. But was the *perilous* shekinah to blame or some flaw in the Dane himself?

Dejon settled back on his chair and refilled his goblet. Moth Fold's acridity might have been Thrisdane's ultimate undoing but, according to Kydane, things had gone awry well before that.

Dejon frowned. Rifts were sensitive to scent and resonance but the effect of the traveler's *emotional* state was less known. Human caste had a greater emotional range than angel caste but some level of predictability was still possible. The emotions of daimon caste should be similarly predictable, even given the breadth of daimon

13

caste manifestations, but what of the emotions of a daimon *with wings*?

Dejon gulped down his ambrosia, barely aware of doing so, as he grappled with the notion of a *winged* daimon. A daimon could only inherit half its substance from its angelic parent and given the dominating weightiness of human caste elements, this equated to far less in reality and certainly not enough to manifest wings. To have wings, a daimon must be *more* than half angel.

Dejon's hand jerked and ambrosia soaked his robe as his mind raced inexorably towards a logical but chilling conclusion. For a daimon to be *more* than half angel, its human caste parent must also be daimon. The possibilities of the Rynth were uncountable but daimon birthing daimon? Surely there had to be another cause. But Dejon knew that had he been embroiled in a debate he would have just been bested for there *was* no other explanation.

Chapter 3

Viv soon lost all track of time. There was no sun to rise and set, no moon to wax and wane, and no stars to spark and die at dawn's bright birthing, for there was no dawn. Nor did she need to break her *days* with sleep or mark them with meals. After her chaotic life in the gangs, when she had slept for days and interspersed near starvation with gorging, the jail's rigid regimen had been unbearable, but now she yearned for something, *anything* to interrupt the monotony, or for *someone*.

How she missed Thris! She had allowed herself to grow used to his easy going company, to his patience, *to his beauty*. Angels did not speak of death but of their essence passing on and Viv wondered bleakly if his exquisite perfume was as scattered as the sand.

By the time a wind stirred, Viv had forgotten her wish for something to break the fold's tedium. It was gentle at first, lifting the sand from the dunes like spray from a wave but as it strengthened, it stirred the sand in the dips as well, until she walked through a hazy, knee-high blanket. The wind continued to grow, whipping more and more sand into the air until it stung like a thousand bites, and Viv wrapped her spare shirt around her head and face.

She struggled on but the wind gusted from all directions, seeming determined to thrust her back no matter which way she turned. It pulled the sand from beneath her feet and was so thick in the air, it was hard to breathe. She needed a rift out but the sand obliterated *everything* and she staggered and fell to her knees. 'Thris,' she gasped. 'Help me.'

Ash jerked upright from the slab. He had dreamed of storming sand before but not of the shekinah trapped by it. He leapt from the slab, wild thoughts of begging aid from Prime-archae Mirek tumbling through his head, but he knew the Prime-archae could not help. Agitation quickened his wings and he blundered against the wall and recoiled as glittering motes erupted from the stone. His shoulder glowed with blue light and Ash beat at it frantically to rid himself of the strange contagion then heard the hum of the resonant music.

The same music had helped him guide Thris from the Helixai's entrapping tunnels and trembling, Ash lay his hands against the wall. The window did not appear and without knowing why, he closed his eyes and exhaled. Had his eyes been open he would have seen the air spark but what he saw instead, was the inside of a rift.

A fold of jungle green appeared at the other end and he willed the storm of sand to appear but the green gave way to blackness instead. He did not inhale, despite his desperation for air, and then when he could endure it no longer, the rift's ending filled with sand and he crumpled to the floor.

Deep in Sand Fold's brutal bluster, Viv sensed an oasis of calm and crawled towards it and then blessedly, she was out of the blasting sand. She was so relieved to breathe again, she did not care where or how she exited the rift, which turned out to be a mistake. She was flung out, bounced once, and came to a stop when her head smacked against stone. Pain ricocheted through her skull and she fought to remain conscious as black blotches threatened her sight. The fold might contain things even deadlier than cat creatures and sand, but the understanding was no match for bone against stone, and the darkness swallowed her.

Roaith en-Leferen perched on an arruk branch and stared down at the prone form. His green eyes never left the Valen but he did not approach, even to snatch some of its bright curly hair. It seemed to sleep but it might be dead. It was hard to tell with the Valen. They roosted on the ground whether well or ill and were often silent.

If it *were* dead, it was fitting it should be here where the Lefer brought their own Quiet Ones. Roaith's chitter sank to a thrum as he bobbed his head respectfully to the four sectors of the Circle of Silence and dutifully contemplated the Lefer who had been lost to the Song. And then, with the obligatory moment of remembrance complete, he turned his attention back to the Valen.

It remained motionless and as the light ebbed and the Song's pitch sank to the sombre timbre of night, the idea the Valen *was* dead lodged in Roaith's mind like a seed memory. The Valen was deep in the trees and Roaith's crest stirred as he wondered whether Garian's cawings were true and the Valens' bickerings *had* driven their kind into the Leferen. Yet, in all the shell memories inherited from the countless hatchings that preceded his, there were none that told of Valen penetrating the margins of the close-packed kirrik, semer and arruk, let alone the Circle of Silence.

The trees were too brittle to climb and the Valen ate the meat of animals that ate the grass of empty places and, apart for the Circle of Silence, there were no empty places in the Leferen. Roaith's soft thrum changed back to a chitter as he pondered whether this Valen was a victim of the skirmishes Garian had warned of but if it were, it did not explain how it came to be *here*.

He cocked his head. It looked female but the sameness of the Valen made it difficult to tell them apart. Perhaps a mate-pair waited for it somewhere. Roaith's *blue* crest and jaw-blade revealed that no mate-pair waited for *him* but he rocked from foot to foot in distress at the possibility of a broken bond.

The darkness deepened and star-sheen intruded to gild the pods that hung in the surrounding trees. Only those that held the most recently interred Lefer remained intact, the older pods having already spilled their cargo of powdery flesh and brittle bones to the forest floor. Not that there was much on the ground to show for it; slo-flies made short work of whatever came their way.

Roaith's head cocked again as he considered whether it were the remains of the Quiet Ones that prevented the trees from growing in the Circle. The Song did not speak of it and nor did the Lefer who, unlike Roaith, lingered here only to farewell their Silent Ones before returning to the Rookery.

Garian disapproved of Roaith's visits but the Circle allowed Roaith to watch the stars blaze in patterns as complex as a slo-fly's wing and it was worth Garian's displeasure for that. But as he stared skywards, black shapes swept overhead to obscure the stars and envelop him in a pungent stench and Roaith clucked in disgust. Night-sliders hunted anything that reached its *Quiet Time* and would return for the Valen's remains. They would leave its hair though, he comforted himself, for night-sliders had no appetite for beauty.

And then the Valen moved. Roaith watched it struggle to its hands and knees, then rest. Its weakness reminded him of a hatchling and as his protective instincts flared, he used his climbing-claws to swing himself down the arruk. But he was less than halfway to the ground when he heard the gruntings of a morrog.

He stopped and his claws gouged the bark as he fought the urge to flee back up the tree. The slow syncopation of grunts told him the morrog had yet to take the Valen's scent, but it would and Roaith chittered in distress. The Valen was as vulnerable as an egg-wet chick and he released his claws and slid to the ground. The morrog would hear him but so would the Valen and, like a chick, might have the wits to copy his method of escape.

The morrog burst into the clearing and Roaith leapt back up the arruk and hauled himself swiftly to its crown. He had no time to see whether the morrog pursued him or the Valen but morrog could not climb so he was safe. The Circle filled with the sound of its fury and Roaith's attention swung to the Valen's hiding place in the kirrik opposite. It had climbed surprisingly high and now risked the kirrik's brittle branches sending it crashing down into the morrog's putrid jaws.

Roaith chittered again, quickly descended to where the branches of his arruk meshed with the neighboring arruk's, sprang across and continued from tree to tree around the Circle of Silence until he reached the Valen's kirrik, and then he climbed.

Chapter 4

Viv locked her arms around the tree's slender trunk and struggled to still the sickening thump of her head. The branches below her rattled as if the pig-bear thing were about to burst through and her brain screamed at her to fly away. But after knocking herself senseless, she doubted she had the skills to clear the trees and if she clipped one, the pig-bear waited.

Huge stinking moths, then bloody cat creatures, and now some hideous thing with the head of a wild pig and the squat body of a bear. Where the hell were all the beautiful things Thris had promised her? The pig-bear had gone quiet but its stink filled the tree and Viv pulled her knees up in case it grabbed her ankles, and then the branches shook.

She stifled a scream but it was the birdman that appeared through the foliage not the pig-bear. She had glimpsed it as the pig-bear had charged and now it was after her too. She looked around wildly for something to defend herself but it simply cocked its head and stared. The starlight revealed a human-shaped body covered in smooth, green feathers but its wings were folds of skin strung between its wrists and hips. It had claws on its elbows and Viv wondered if it were really a *batman* rather than a birdman.

Its face shared the reassuring chubbiness of a budgie's and it looked more curious than hostile but just as her fear ebbed, it flapped its membranous wings and she gave a terrified squeal. It ignored her, intent on the sky and she risked a glance upwards. She had thought the coloured stars of the cat creature's fold extraordinary but the stars here were so bright they cast shadows.

The birdman's face was too birdlike to show human emotions but Viv sensed its love for the stars in its soft trill. Nothing suggested it was worried about the pig-bear and there was no sound of anything creeping up the tree, just a low wash of chirrups from the forest, which was odd given birds roosted at night.

She relaxed her grip on the branch and rubbed her aching knuckles. She was probably safe in the trees but she had a crappy feeling she was not going to find a rift in the branches, then again, she did not know enough about rifts to be certain, having been content to let Thris run the show. Viv grimaced. She had been Jimmy Wright's punching-bag and Rim's plaything; the passive *client* of countless government agencies and the criminal delinquent of the legal system; and then the *package* Thris was to deliver to earn his Brownie points for ascension.

Hard to break the habits of a lifetime, eh Vivi? Rim's voice intruded. Viv swore and the birdman's head swiveled. 'I don't suppose you know how to speak English?' she asked sarcastically. The birdman cocked its head and its crest rose slightly. 'I didn't think so, but if you did, I was going to ask you for directions to the nearest rift.'

The birdman ruffled its feathers and then with a swift hop, disappeared through the foliage. Viv did not know whether to feel relieved or dismayed and was wondering whether to pursue it when it reappeared, stared at her, and repeated the trick. Viv was heartily sick of being alone and despite feeling like an actor in a B-grade movie where a dog barks a message, she edged after it. The birdman glanced back as it hopped onto a neighboring tree and Viv cautiously climbed across, still woozy from the crack to the head.

The birdman led her from tree to tree and as the clearing disappeared behind a wall of close-packed trunks, Viv wondered whether she was a fool to leave the rift behind. There were worse things than being with the birdman, especially at night, she supposed. It knew where the dangers lurked and would avoid them unless *it* was the danger.

Viv shrugged off the thought. Predatory birds had tearing beaks and the birdman's was more like a canary's, then again, it might use its elbow claws to carve up its meals. Darker blobs appeared among the trees but unlike the pods at the clearing, these were nests. It must be some sort of rookery, she concluded, then the birdman cheeped and hopped down several branches to a nest.

It looked identical to the others: shaped like a teardrop and woven from greenwood, twigs, and leaves. The birdman disappeared through the circular opening then popped its head out and trilled. The invitation was unmistakable but Viv wondered whether the nest held the bones of its previous guests and she nervously glanced at the night-shrouded trees.

She needed to sleep off her dizziness and huddling on a branch was not going to do it so she eased herself through the opening. The branch creaked ominously and she held her breath but nothing gave way and she carefully lowered herself down. The birdman rustled around in the dimness as it settled for the night and as its wing brushed her and she recoiled, her foot connected with something solid. She jerked her feet up. The last thing she wanted was to break the birdman's eggs.

She hugged herself as she lay in the darkness and the more she considered how little she knew of the creature, the more she regretted climbing into its nest. But her head ached and the nest was as soft as a feather bed. Like floating on a cloud, she thought vaguely, and drifted into sleep.

In the highest nest in the Rookery, Garian roused. The Song went on as before but he exited his nest and his blood-red crest came erect as his sharp eyes searched the darkness. All seemed in order but he sensed his domain had been invaded and, with a caw of fury, he took to the air.

Deep in the Blue Helixai, Ash came to his senses slowly then started as he noticed Ky standing grim-faced beside the slab. Ash's heart quickened. 'Have the Principae sent?' he asked.

'No.'

'Then there is a chance Thris still lives.'

'Do you really believe that?'

'Have you seen Archae Dejon?' asked Ash, looking at Ky closely.

'Yes. He instructed me to tell no one of what happened. What did Prime-archae Mirek say?'

'Very little. He—'

Ky's face twisted and Ash recoiled. 'It is the shekinah's fault, not Thris's! It was *she* who tempted him, like she tempted me in Crystal Fold!'

'Tempted you?'

'She touched me . . . offered me her mouth. She would have offered me more had I not pulled away.'

Ash shook his head. 'Thris cared for her in Ezam and resisted all temptation. You told me yourself how bitter Moth Fold was. It was that which—'

'No! I saw her breasts! She would have flaunted them at Thris too!' Ash did not want to make things worse by arguing but the dream had been clear. The shekinah had sought aid in Moth Fold not seduction. 'She is unnatural even for a daimon,' continued Ky harshly. 'She has wings, bronze like her hair.'

Ash gasped. 'Are you saying she is Iahhel?'

'I am saying she is perilous! She has destroyed Thris and she will destroy me!'

Tart vapor fumed from Ky's skin and Ash struggled not to recoil. 'Have you rested since you spoke to your mentor?'

'How can I rest when . . .' Ky's voice cracked and he wiped his arm across his face.

'Rest here,' said Ash. He slid from the slab and leaned in subtly so his breath dusted the other angel. 'I will play for you.'

'I do not like this cavern,' muttered Ky, but he allowed Ash to help him onto the slab and lay down. Ash usually played with his eyes closed but this time he watched Ky and only when Ky had calmed did he consider Ky's extraordinary claim. Angels could not lie *consciously* but seeing Thris torn apart might have distorted Ky's senses. Yet his description of the shekinah's wings had been very precise: *bronze, like her hair*.

If she were a winged daimon, she must be placed amongst those closest to her own state and yet even an Archae on the verge of transcendence could not discharge such a duty. The Tome was explicit that rifts denied passage between Ezam and Erath, *except* that as a new Dane, Ash had ended up there.

Ash's playing faltered as he wondered whether his *accidental* visit to the Iahhel's fold was linked to his

24

experiences in the Blue Helixai. He knew of no angels who suffered waking dreams although they might hide the fact, but what could not be hidden were the white feathers of ascension in his wings.

Ash brought his wings forward and was mortified to discover even more snowy plumage. Prime-archae Mirek warned the Helixai might resent his intrusion and deny him ascension but the opposite seemed true. The Prime-archae also said there was no evil in Ezam except what an angel carried in his heart. The understanding comforted Ash and his thoughts turned to the absent member of their threesome. 'Come back to us, Thris,' he murmured. 'Come back to those who love you.'

Chapter 5

Thris drifted in a starry abyss, his consciousness strung out like beads on a wire. He yearned for the wire to break, for the beads to scatter, for the dissolution necessary to integration with the Great Beyond, but the wire held him and, with infinite slowness, drew him back together.

Thris raged against the loss of the Great Beyond, at being denied its grace, at the agony of his reconstitution. He screamed as flesh wove back onto bones, as blood burned through his veins, as skin tightened its grip on him, keeping him intact. But worse still were the memories inserted back into his brain and trapped there by the bones of his skull, to remind him endlessly of his cataclysmic failure.

The pain had dulled by the time he opened his eyes in Crystal Fold's tinselly meadow and he winced as the silvery glare assaulted his senses. For a moment he thought himself blind, then the sky faded to mauve and someone loomed over him. It was Ash, his face so full of tenderness that tears slid from Thris's eyes, warm against his skin.

Ash spoke, but his voice was distant, like sound had been when Thris had first woken in Ezam. I am new, he thought vaguely, then confusion swamped him as shattered memories drifted back. He had run and swum and flown; competed in trials and come to win them; been gifted an Archae's trust and betrayed it. He was not new at all.

He wanted to protest as Ash's strong arms gathered him up but speech was beyond him, as was keeping his eyes open. Air pulsed about him, rousing more broken memories that slipped away before he grasped them.

He yearned to slip away too but awareness surged back bringing with it a monstrous pain.

Breathing was agony, his ribs cracking with every breath, and while he had been mute before, now he roared. Sweet clouds of scent brought moments of respite but it was not enough and he fought to escape into death.

Ky pressed back against the window frame as far from Thris as possible while obedient to Ash's exhortation to keep watch. Ky had flung the window shutters wide to rid the room of citrus, but Thris sloughed it in sickening waves and Ky gulped down the outside air as if he drowned.

The Dendrinai glittered below as usual and the murmur of angelic debate drifted up from Haven's portico as it always did and yet Ezam was utterly changed. He had been overjoyed to learn Thris had been gifted back and had imagined Thris would be the same as before but while Thris bore no signs of his terrible injuries, his pain was so great they bound him to the bed to stop him hurling himself from the balcony.

Nor was that the worst of it. Ky sensed a terrible change in Thris, as if Thris's flawless exterior hid a hollow core, and he wondered whether the Principae had punished Thris by keeping his most precious part for themselves. The notion contradicted everything he knew of the Principae but he struggled to refute it.

The Principae oversaw the trials that drove Dane to the edge of endurance but never to the ruination of their perfection. It was incomprehensible they would damage an angel in this way. Ky's face hardened as he gripped the window frame. Thris's injury did not stem from the

Principae, he concluded, but from the shekinah, a malign element even beyond the Principaes' ken.

Neither Crystal nor Ezam Folds held female-aspected angels so even the learned did not know how they corrupted the Host. Prime-archae Serith's strident warnings had not helped; so repetitive the Host had reacted with polite amusement *until* the appearance of the Black Obsidian Stele and then had avoided the topic altogether.

Ky jumped as Ash alighted on the balcony with his lyre and while he smiled at Ky, he went straight to Thris's bedside. Ky's distressed gaze followed him and anger replaced horror at the sight of Ash's white plumage. Not only had the shekinah caused Thris's injuries but she had pushed Ash closer to ascension by triggering his extraordinary dash through the rifts. If Ash ascended and Thris died, Ky would be left alone.

Ash was intent on his music and Ky launched from the balcony and powered away. A trio of new Dane tested their wings further afield but it was unlikely they had manifested in Ezam as a threesome like he, Ash and Thris. It required three Archae to simultaneously transcend to Crystal Fold and three Principae to simultaneously pass onto the glorious Great Beyond.

The aberration of his own arrival added to his turmoil and he gave the Dane a wide berth and sped away over the Hollow Hills. The Thorny Mountains loomed with its Blue Helixai and as he swerved away, he caught sight of the Red. Its distant glow reminded him of happier, *simpler* times and he turned his wings in its direction.

He had always thought the Red Helixai superior to the Blue, Ash's favourite, and to the White which Thris admired and they had debated the Helixais' merits until he and Thris had been blessed with mentors and turned their attention to more important matters.

The twisted red mountain had lost none of its impact, its pulses of gold, vermillion and crimson flame reminiscent of the Carnelian Stele. Like the Blue, the Red Helixai was peppered with openings and he landed and stalked inside. Fire-plumes threw red shadows against the walls, as raw as his emotions, and his anger grew.

He had heard that fire was common in Moonsun Fold where it spat black smoke like human caste spat waste. Why had the Great Beyond created human caste at all, let alone as a parody of the Host? Human caste decayed, practiced deceit, were prone to violence. They were worse than Redice bears for at least those beasts resembled their vile natures.

He strode back to the cavern's entrance and sped away over the Dendrinai, using anger to power his flight until he sensed an ambrosia font below then he angled sharply and sliced through the canopy. The ferocity of his entry tore branches from the glis and his wings still beat violently as he scooped handfuls of the fragrant liquid to his mouth, but he was not alone.

'Kydane,' said Archae Kald pleasantly. 'Just the angel I hoped to see.'

Ash had never played his lyre beyond the Blue Helixai and he hoped that in some small way, it might aid Thris's healing. He poured all his love and tenderness into his music and as he played, he wondered why the Principae had left Thris's healing incomplete. Perhaps their intention was to reveal important insights, but if so, what?

After a time he noticed his music seemed to affect Thris's breathing. Some harmonies soothed Thris better than others and he was concentrating on finding the most powerful melodies when Archae Kald suddenly burst into the room.

Ash managed to bow but the Archae knocked him aside as he strode to the bed. Ash's heart hammered as the Archae seemed about to wrench Thris from the covers but stopped just short. Even so, Thris's breathing grew as ragged as if the Archae *had* seized him.

'He is unaware,' said Ash hoarsely.

'You will send him to me *immediately* he *is* aware,' the Archae said, his glare as brutal as the Black Obsidian Stele. 'Is that understood, Dane?'

'Yes, Archae.' Instinct clamped Ash's wings close to his back and as the door slammed shut, he gripped the bedhead to stay upright. There was a new odour in the room, as metallic as blood, and Ash's terrified gaze went to Thris before he realised the stench was anger. 'But the Archae have transcended such base emotions,' he whispered, and then the shocking understanding struck him that it might be possible for angels to slide back down the hierarchy.

Chapter 6

Viv was woken by a thunderous wash of birdsong. It was as if a thousand church bells pealed, all with different timbres. She kept her eyes closed, hoping to recapture sleep, but the clamor was too loud. Some birdcalls were low like drumbeats and others celestial but after a while the cacophony settled into a choir, the harmonies so precise Viv imagined a birdman with a conductor's baton clutched in its claw.

She suppressed a grin and cautiously opened her eyes. She was alone. A dusty shaft of light streamed in from the nest's opening to illuminate a curious collection of objects at her feet. What she had thought was an egg last night was a silver cup, beautifully etched with curling lines. There were scraps of silver metal too, a belt buckle, a ring of metal attached to a leather stub, a bronze-coloured nail with a flattened head, a single red wooden bead, and some shreds of red yarn.

It was like a bowerbird's nest except bowerbirds thieved blue things. They did so to attract mates and given her experience with the cat creature, Viv decided it was time to be on her way. She grabbed her pack and shuffled towards the entrance on her backside, reluctant to risk her human feet punching holes in the nest, got to her knees, and peered out. There was no sign of the birdman or others of its kind and she eased herself out onto a branch and pulled on the pack.

A breeze scattered sunlight through the branches and Viv drew the fragrant air deep into her lungs. She could almost be in the gum trees at the back of her childhood house. She had climbed into them, sometimes in the dead

31

of night, old enough to know they made her feel safe but not old enough to know why.

Viv's mouth twisted. It was no use dwelling on how things might have been had Kald *not* knocked-up her mother, Viv *not* decided a car accident was a good way to quit her shitty life, and a pack of stinking grubs had *not* turned Thris into an arsehole. What she had to do *now* was to climb clear of the canopy and fly to where a rift might be so she could continue the search for her mother.

But as she gripped the branch above to swing herself up, it snapped off and crashed away through the foliage to the ground. Viv swallowed dryly and tested another with the same result. The branch she stood on was scarcely thicker and heart in her mouth, she inched along it to the next tree, chose a sturdy-looking branch, and gingerly stepped across.

She continued from tree to tree, careful to test each branch, before she stepped onto it. The trees brittleness was odd but given Ezam's trees were metallic and Moth Fold's dun-coloured, she supposed their fragility should not be surprising.

Occasionally the foliage shook as if something passed overhead but Viv saw no more birdmen or anything else for that matter. She should be grateful, she supposed, having seen many strange things since that sweltering day in the cemetery, including purple-eyed angels. Not strange, one of the *uncountable possibilities* of the Rynth, she amended sarcastically, like a daimon. Rim would have called her *an effing freak* but Thris had insisted daimon were simply different rather than inferior to angels.

She had not believed him then and she did not believe him now. Angels had no need to eat or crap or pee and did not suffer from cancer or bung knees. And they were beautiful. Even Kald, whose features were honed by arrogance, had a glorious majesty.

Whereas daimon . . . She would live longer than a human, but how much longer? And how would she age? And how long would that old age last? She did not want to be decrepit for centuries and if she chose the wrong fold, she would not be, hunted down as soon as her unnaturalness showed. Terrifying as the future seemed, it might have been bearable had she been with Thris.

He is dead, forget him, she admonished herself. She would be with her mother instead, she insisted, but as she gazed at the endless mesh of branches, that future seemed unlikely too.

Viv grew more and more frustrated as the day wore on. The canopy remained impenetrable and she dreaded spending the night fumbling about in the dark. The pig-bear had attacked at dusk and she guessed it and its mates were probably more active at night. Desperate to get her bearings, she finally risked climbing higher, broke a hole through the canopy, and peered out.

The view confirmed her worst fears. The trees were all at different heights which meant she would have to fly straight up to clear them. She had seen Thris, Ash and Ky do exactly that but she had never tried it herself. Sand Fold had been open and she had only learned to take off and land at an angle *and* to pick up speed slowly.

Then something swooped overhead and she flinched. It was another birdman, bigger than the first and red-crested. It passed over again, lower this time and Viv recoiled as it glared straight at her through the broken foliage. The first birdman had been curious but this one was definitely hostile. And then, with an ear-splitting screech, it crashed through the branches.

Viv dived behind the trunk as its elbow claws slashed and it screeched in frustration as it tried to reach her. Another birdman appeared, attracted by the fracas *or* by the chance of a meal, and then several more.

Viv leapt down to a lower a branch but a birdman's claws snagged her hair and with a burning wrench tore out a clump. Viv had no time to dwell on the pain. She snapped off a branch and spun, using it as a weapon to defend herself but the birdmen had not followed. The group remained on the higher bow in a loose circle around the red-crested birdman and the robber of her hair.

The red-crested birdman had puffed out its chest but the thief refused to relinquish its prize and the red-crested birdman launched, elbow claws slashing. The thief dropped the hair on the branch between them and launched too and a fight broke out. The birdmen shrieked and slashed and as blood splattered the leaves around her, the rats of memories stirred.

There had been blood on the lino at home when Jimmy Wright had beaten her mother and blood on the squats' soiled carpets when the gangs had brawled. Viv knew she should slip away but she felt too numb. She had read that people got used to anything, even living in concentration camps, but she had never got used to violence. Perhaps her angel part prevented her becoming hardened to it, as it prevented her from lying.

The hair-thief was clearly losing the fight and knowing the battle must soon end, spurred Viv into action. She wrenched off her pack, stuffed her jacket, shirt and chemise inside, secured it to her waist and unbedded her wings. She would have a better chance of escaping without the pack but it held things she needed *and* Thris's precious feathers.

The shrieking stopped and Viv feared she had left her escape too late but the birdmen's attention was still on the combatants. The thief backed away along the branch, head down, wings trailing and the red-crested birdman followed, all strut and puffed chest but it did not attack. It kept pace with its vanquished foe until the defeated birdman exited backwards through the circle of watchers then hastened back, scooped up her hair, and cawed in triumph.

Viv seized the moment to launch skywards and had rocketed past the victor before its boastful trumpet had finished. A gleaming peak floated above the clouds but she had no time to wonder at it, just streaked away downslope, a posse of birdmen in pursuit.

The red-crested bully led as it flew higher and faster than the rest and Viv forced herself to greater speed but a glance over her shoulder revealed the bully had closed the gap. And then astonishingly, one of its wings collapsed and it cartwheeled across the sky and crashed back through the canopy. Viv had an instant to wonder at its demise before the forest below her abruptly came to an end and a stinging pain erupted in her shoulder.

A reed had embedded itself in her flesh but as numbness spread, she realised it was far more sinister. She wrenched it out but could no longer feel her left wing and instinctively threw herself back into the shelter of the trees. Her head swam and she felt the smack of twigs and the shock of snapping branches as she fell to earth.

Thoughts of pig-bears sent a burst of panic but her arms were too heavy to lift, let alone grab a passing branch and then her descent was halted so violently her head whiplashed back against a trunk. The impact was far away too and Viv was dimly aware her body dangled like a ragdoll *or* a piece of pig-bear bait before that awareness was lost as well.

Chapter 7

Dejon strode about his rooms too angry to harmonise. Dane were subservient to higher angelic orders but an Archae's mentoring relationship excluded interference from *all* others, especially the kind of brutal interrogation Kald had subjected Kydane to.

Kydane had been incoherent by the time he had stumbled into the portico's shelter and had needed physical support to reach Dejon's rooms. Dejon's only comfort was that despite Kald's coercion, he had failed to discover the single most important fact, namely, that the shekinah was winged.

Dejon's own questioning of his protégé had been hampered by Kald's earlier interrogation and it had taken Dejon a long time to extract exactly what Kald had learned. Kydane now rested in the next room, safe from Kald's meddling, not that Dejon thought Kald would bother with the lowly Dane again. Such was his arrogance, Kald believed he had discovered *everything* of importance.

Kald now knew of Kydane's role of Shadow and of the difficulties that had beset Thrisdane's Guideship, but his questioning had ceased when he had learned of Moth Fold's acridity. In uncovering what he believed to be the cause of his protégé's failure, Kald believed he had discovered the means to salvage his protégé's ascension *and* his own transcendence, and so it would seem.

The Principae knew Moth Fold's foul stench would even compromise an Archae and that an imperfect Dane would be completely undone. They also knew Thrisdane had sacrificed himself to save the shekinah, an act worthy of ascension for himself *and* of transcendence for his mentor but Kald had overlooked that because, for all Thrisdane's selflessness, the Guideship remained uncompleted.

Not only had Kald failed in his duty to unite the shekinah with her mother but the Dane *Kald* had chosen to discharge *his* responsibility, was now barely aware of himself, let alone his obligations. Dejon smiled grimly. If Kald sought to share in the rewards of his protégé's accomplishments, then he must also share in his protégé's failures.

Dejon paused to down two goblets of ambrosia in quick succession and harmonise, then brought his attention to the more *subtle* effects of Kald's failures. The Host were duty bound to avoid disturbing the Rynth, a responsibility discharged through their own actions and the actions of those they influenced. As part of these obligations, Dejon had brought his concerns about the shekinah to Kald's attention, *and been rebuffed*, as had Prime-archae Mirek.

They had acted as they should, as had Kydane, who had rendered Thrisdane and the shekinah aid in extraordinarily dangerous circumstances. Kydane had also communicated to Thrisdane Dejon's warning of anomalies in the shekinah's resonance, again to no avail.

Dejon refused to stoop to the tawdry practice of tallying his acts of virtue against those of his fellow Archae but could not help noticing that while the Principae had few things to commend Kald for, his own list of accomplishments continued to grow.

Dejon sipped a third goblet of ambrosia more calmly and settled on his plushly cushioned chair. Kald would order Thrisdane back out into the Rynth far sooner than the damaged Dane could accommodate, in fact, given Kydane's description of the Dane's injuries, Dejon doubted Thrisdane would ever regain his former strength.

Not that Kald would be deterred. His only concern would be to please the Principae by delivering the shekinah to her mother as swiftly as possible.

Dejon also predicted that the difficulties that plagued Thrisdane's Guideship would continue, given the shekinah's nature remained unchanged, and that in his weakened state, Thrisdane would be even less likely to cope with them. In fact, the Guideship had a far smaller chance of success now than it had before. Dejon smiled as he considered how Thrisdane's demise would elevate Kydane and further enhance Dejon's journey to transcendence. The prospect was very pleasing indeed.

Ash came to ground close to the Bokos and bedded his wings. It was an uncomfortable process, as if they had outgrown their space or the space had been filled by something else. He dismissed the worrying idea, relieved to have his white plumage safely hidden. Thris was well enough to leave for a short time and Ash had been forced to because Ky had disappeared.

Ky was still distressed by Thris's injury and Ash would keep his visit to Prime-archae Mirek short but as he hurried through the Bokos's dim interior, it was Prime-archae Serith he stumbled upon. Ash bowed and palmed but struggled to hide his shock. Serith's face was gaunt and his hair completely silver. Even more disconcerting was the Prime-archae's gaze, that continued on Ash well after Ash had completed his formal greeting.

'Only one blue angel is gifted to Ezam at any time,' murmured Serith. 'You must be Ashdane.'

'Yes, Prime-archae,' said Ash, dismayed by the revelation. Dane only gathered in numbers at trials and then their focus was on winning. Ash had never noticed the absence of other blues before.

'Mirek has spoken of you,' the Prime-archae continued, 'and I have shown him the scrolls that speak of your kind.'

Ash thanked him shakily and wondered whether scrolls spoke ill of *his kind* and whether Prime-archae Mirek would still welcome his company. Then again, the scrolls might give explanation for the white in his wings. Perhaps blue pigment was rare because it leached out to give the *appearance* of early ascension.

Ash was considering this encouraging possibility when Prime-archae Mirek appeared. The Prime-archae's smile was genuine, noted Ash in relief, and after Mirek had exchanged pleasantries with Serith, he led Ash away. They passed empty shelves Ash had not noticed before and he stared at them curiously.

'Presumably, they have been left free for new angel lore,' said Mirek, noticing his interest. 'Although it seems we have added nothing new for eons. It is as if Ezam's learning has come to a halt.' They settled at a table near a window but the light struggled to pierce the shadows and Ash thought longingly of the bright air outside. 'I am guessing you have not come here to enjoy the Bokos's views,' said Mirek dryly. 'Has something occurred you wish to discuss?'

'Yes Prime-archae. As you know, I have been caring for Thris, and while he is no longer in pain, he is far from healed. Archae Kald has visited. He was . . . *upset* and ordered . . .' Ash stopped, not having intended to speak so disrespectfully.

'That Thrisdane present himself to the Archae before you believe Thrisdane is fully restored?' finished Mirek.

Ash dipped his head. 'Is that all that troubles you, Ashdane?'

'Archae Kald also spoke to Ky and Ky was . . . *disturbed* by the interview and is still distressed by Thris's injuries. If Thris is to continue his Guideship, then Ky must leave too and he is unpractised in transiting.'

Given the Dane's frankness, Mirek was not surprised Ashdane now looked everywhere but him, but it was what the blue angel had only hinted at that was most revealing. Kald had discovered Thrisdane's return and was not only furious but insistent Thrisdane immediately complete the Guideship. He had also interrogated Kydane to discover the reasons for the Guideship's failure to ensure they were not repeated.

Mirek smoothed his robe as if its neatness were his only concern but his thoughts were anything but ordered. Kald must know how fine a line he trod between serving his own interests and damaging them, and imposing his will on another Archae's protégé breached protocols auspiced by the Principae themselves. *And* it seemed Kald would now force a Dane, whose essence remained damaged, from Ezam's safety. The Principae might not intervene in Ezam's affairs but they watched and they judged.

Ashdane had come to him for advice but what was he to say? Do not dare to question the Archae who are your superiors in every way? Be satisfied that if Archae Kald delays the ascension of your friends, his own transcendence will also be impeded?

'When Thris and Ky leave Ezam, I am going too,' said Ashdane abruptly.

Mirek felt an uncomfortable thud in his chest, the sensation so unfamiliar it took him a moment to realise it was fear. The scrolls confirmed blue angels were rare and given Ashdane's astonishing abilities *and* gentle nature, Mirek was keen he not be risked.

'You are unpractised in transiting,' he said, 'and despite your feat in bringing Thrisdane back, the rifts are dangerous, as events have shown. I believe you would be more help to your friends if you stayed here.'

'I *will* go with them,' repeated Ashdane, 'for they *will* need my aid.'

Ashdane's certainty triggered a second thud in Mirek's chest and he wondered if the Dane had experienced another episode of prescience. 'You can provide aid from the safety of Ezam, as you have already demonstrated,' he persisted.

'No, I . . .' said Ashdane, then dropped his head.

As well he might, thought Mirek dazedly. The blue angel had actually *argued* with him! Ezam's hierarchy created explicit expectations of respect and obligation and while the Archaes' proximity to the Great Beyond granted them dominion over the lower orders, it also obliged them to guide and protect those orders. Ashdane's thinly veiled criticisms breached these protocols but so did Archae Kald's dealings with Thrisdane and Kydane, as did his *own* questioning of the Archae's behaviour.

'I am sorry, Prime-archae,' said Ashdane miserably.

'I am not sure you need be,' said Mirek faintly, and wondered whether blue angels were harbingers of change. It would explain why Ezam could tolerate only one at a time given the risk of even one tearing Ezam's fabric to shreds. Ashdane's head was still bowed and Mirek retrieved two scrolls from the shelf behind him and set them on the table. 'Prime-archae Serith believes the rarity of blue angels is significant,' he said. 'Read, Ashdane.'

Ashdane obediently smoothed out the scrolls but his gaze remained on the parchment long after he had finished reading and it was Mirek who was first to speak. 'So as you see, Ashdane, there is at least one other instance of early ascension of a blue angel.'

'I do not mean to question you, Prime-archae, but might it simply be a coincidence that the angel *Sen*, who also had white plumage as a Dane, just happened to be blue?'

'Senquar-archae's colour might have been inconsequential to what happened *or* crucial,' said Mirek. 'Whatever the case, it should ease your mind to know there is a precedent for early ascension.' Ashdane nodded but Mirek could see the Dane was anything but at ease.

'I thank you for your words, Prime-archae,' he said. 'With your permission, I must return to Haven. I have left Thris alone too long and I must find Ky.'

Mirek nodded but the blue angel had reminded him of something else Ashdane had in common with Senquar-archae. Like Ashdane, Senquar-archae had blinked into existence in Ezam not alone, as was usual, but in the company of two other angels.

Chapter 8

The sky had cycled through peach and umber many times before Thris left his bed and set out for the Halls. He went slowly, having to rest at regular intervals and barely able to detour around feasting lacewings. Ky's resonance told him the Shadow hovered beyond the glis but at least Thris had escaped Ash's vigilance. Knowing how unworthy he was made the blue angel's love yet another burden to bear.

Thris's betrayal of his mentor crouched in the space where his heart had been and with every pulse, sent despair spewing deep into his angelic being. Archae Kald would strip Thris of the Guideship and Ky assume the mantle that the Principae, in their wisdom, had intended, but if only that were all! Thris staggered to a stop and buried his face in his hands. Ky's lack of transiting skills would imperil Ky as well as the shekinah and Thris's betrayal circle wide to include their destruction as well.

The glis leaves stirred but their music was as discordant to his ears as the rattle that preceded human caste death. Human caste feared death but Thris longed to be unshackled from flesh and feather and merge at last with the infinite sweetness of the Great Beyond. And how close he had come! If only the Principae had not returned him to Ezam, broken open with his flaws revealed for all to see.

He would never again be strong enough to compete in trials or develop the skills to ascend by other means. All that was left was to use the last of his strength to help Ky complete the Guideship and ascend. The understanding was bitter-sweet but it was enough for him to trudge on.

Ash's anxiety over Ky's whereabouts was exacerbated by Thris's disappearance from Haven. He redoubled his fruitless sweeps over the Dendrinai and Hollow Hills and in desperation, returned to the Blue Helixai, sprinted along the tunnel and laid his palms against the stone. The window appeared and breathless, he peered in.

The image was clear enough to see the gem-like colours of the lacewings Thris passed in the Dendrinai but Thris was indistinct and Ash's heart missed as he realised the Helixai revealed Thris's *essence* and it was as shadowy as a Moonsun night. Hardly daring to breathe, Ash followed Thris into the Halls and along the Halls' passageways into Archae Kald's rooms and though he trembled at his temerity, he refused to look away.

In contrast to Thris's fragility, Archae Kald's essence glittered like the frosted grass of Crystal Fold and although no sound leaked from the room, Ash knew exactly what was said. There was to be no forgiveness for Thris, no kindness and no understanding, just a command to immediately complete the Guideship.

But that was not all. The Archae warned of the shekinah's likely reluctance to place herself back in Thris's care and ordered Thris to take control of her *by whatever means necessary.* Ash reeled in confusion as his phallus hardened and then realised the Helixai had delivered the *intent* of the Archae's words and his body had understood it first.

The Archae's command to use seduction threw Ash into disjoint and he stumbled back up the tunnel in search of a pool to align. He had not harmonised *consciously* for countless cycles and when he finally became aware of his surroundings again, sensed something had changed. He raced back to the window in the stone but it had disappeared and he sped on to the cavern's entrance and launched into the air. He searched for Thris's resonance as he streaked over the Dendrinai and opened himself as if he communed with the Principae.

The onslaught of resonance from the Host tossed him about like a leaf in the wind and he struggled to steady. Dane were there along with all levels of Archae and at least two steles, but not the precious resonance he sought. He flew on and then blessedly, Ky's print emerged and the telltale vibration of a rift.

Ash angled sharply and crashed through the canopy but was too late to stop Ky blinking out of sight. Knowing he followed Thris, Ash launched himself into the rift, landed with a thump on his belly and scrambled upright. He had entered a strange fold naked with his wings unbedded and he was still blue! Coloured angels manifested as white or black in other folds and then he noticed the glis. He was still in Ezam!

Ash spun back to the rift but it had closed. The Principae had obviously decided he needed to be better equipped for rift travel and he raced back to Haven where clothing from other folds was stored. But donning it proved difficult. Thris had not complained about wearing trousers but Ash found lacing them at the back impossible, as was reaching behind him to button the shirt. At least leaving it unfastened kept his wings free. The boots were so uncomfortable he abandoned them after a few strides and leapt skywards barefoot.

He landed where the rift had been and paced about hoping it would open and when it did not, took to the air again. He sensed for rifts the length and breadth of the Dendrinai, then searched the Hollow Hills and the Thorny Mountains, resting when exhaustion claimed him and guzzling ambrosia when he came across a font. Then, as the umber sky sheened back to peach, he flapped miserably back to the Blue Helixai, staggered inside and collapsed on the slab.

Thris did not have the strength to visit the Keeper at Hearth Fold despite the rift opening close to the small cottage. Instead he offered up thanks to her and to the Great Beyond for the new rift that dilated nearby, and stepped into it. He knew it exited in Moth Fold but the surest way to find the shekinah was to retrace his steps.

The rift delivered him into trees in Moth Fold's dark cycle and he crawled into a hollow and curled up. He had no idea whether it was the same forest he had visited with the shekinah for his mind was sometimes so blank he thought himself new. And yet, as he huddled among the roots, the idea that Ezam's angelic hierarchy could be scaled more than once, floated into his head.

The notion was so bizarre he pondered whether it sprang from the madness of his near dissolution. It suggested the Great Beyond gave angels the chance to make better, *wiser* decisions and he wondered dully whether, given the opportunity, he *would* make wiser decisions. It had been here under Moth Fold's trees he had nearly been overwhelmed by the shekinah's scent and resonance and yet had believed he could control his want of her. It had been an act of arrogance that had cost him everything.

The moths stirred in their roosts and Thris tensed as something threaded its way through the trees towards him. He lacked the strength to stand, let alone fight, and then he all but swooned in relief as he saw it was Ky.

Ky came to a stop and dropped his pack. 'We need to travel together,' he said.

'Our roles preclude that,' said Thris and faltered as he remembered having used the phrase before. Hope flared as he wondered whether he *were* to be granted a second chance at ascension but then the magnitude of his violation slammed home and hope evaporated.

'My task, like yours, is to ensure the Guideship is completed,' said Ky urgently. 'We have a greater chance if we work together.

Thris did not have the strength to argue and Ky crouched in front of him. 'You are not yet recovered, Thris. You are putting yourself in danger!'

'That is . . . not ... your concern.'

'I will *not* risk the shekinah destroying you a second time,' hissed Ky.

'The shekinah is not to blame . . . for my flaws,' panted Thris. 'In appointing you Shadow . . . the Principae . . . recognised them.'

'They recognised your *virtues* in restoring you to us!'

Ky's sweet scent reminded Thris how Ky had tended him in Sand Fold and his heart contracted. 'My dear friend,' he murmured.

'There are things you do not know,' said Ky urgently. 'Things that caused your undoing.' He caught Thris's hand. 'The shekinah has wings.' Thris blinked as he groped for meaning and found none. A daimon's ethereal aspect was *always* subsumed by the heavier elements of its non-angelic parent. A daimon could not have wings. 'I saw them in Beast Fold,' continued Ky eagerly, 'before the beastman attacked you. Do you not see, Thris? She is like the Iahhel. No angel can resist the Iahhel. None of it was your fault.'

She is like the Iahhel. Thris's ravaged brain latched onto the single phrase. To bend a daimon to his will through

48

seduction was shameful enough but to coerce an Iahhel! He would be condemned to Ezam for time uncounted. Ash and Ky would pass on and be lost to him, as would other Dane who might befriend him. He would be like the Thorny Mountains: a witness to the flow of angels towards the Great Beyond but never part of it and if the shekinah *were* Iahhel, his mentor must know it, for Archae Kald knew all.

Chapter 9

Viv dreamed she swung on the monkey-bars at school, her thin legs looped over steel made shiny by countless other legs as she watched the strange, inverted world rock to and fro. But there was no shriek of children at play and she was cold, so cold.

Pain gnawed at her belly and as nausea rose in sweaty waves, she opened her eyes. Her surroundings were so dim she thought she only dreamed opening them and then her befuddled brain pieced together the events that preceded her plunge through the trees.

Her pack strap had snagged a branch and she hung upside down, her wings dangling beneath her. Visions of pig-bears filled her head and she bedded them in an instant but it was a hell of a lot harder to right herself.

She flailed a numb hand at the branch above, missed it, tried again and missed again. Her pack strap cut into her belly and hoping to God the strap did not unhook, she pushed herself away from the tree and as she swung back, threw her leg over the branch and hauled herself after it. She was shaky but the pressure on her belly eased and the nausea with it.

She rested for a while then pulled on her clothing and the thicker jacket Thris had packed for her, and inched along the branch until her back was hard up against the trunk, then rested again, gripping Thris's feather for comfort. The red-crested birdman was probably in some hunter's cooking-pot by now or its head hacked off as a trophy and she felt sorry for it, despite its attack.

Wild creatures acted as Nature dictated, unlike humans, or maybe humans acted true to type too. They had choices though. Even in her miserable life with Jimmy Wright and later in the gangs, there had been choices. It was just that she had made really, really shitty ones.

Viv snuggled deeper into the jacket and caught the faintest whiff of sweetness. If only she and Thris had not ended up in that putrid cave, they could have … *What, Vivi? Had the big white weddin' and ya now be keepin' house for ya angel-man?*

Rim's sarcastic voice rubbed her nose in the truth as it always had. Being only half an angel was never going to be enough for Thris but being a full angel like the mysterious Iahhel probably was not going to be enough either. Thris's path to heaven had been paved with the *absence* of sex *until* she had destroyed it. *Yes, Vivi, add ya name to the long list of evil temptresses: Eve, Delilah, Jezebel.*

Viv scowled. Those were stories written by men to excuse their fears and foibles. She had read somewhere that history was written by the victors and she could well imagine what Jimmy Wright's version of events would read like *and* Kald's. But what would Lettie Wright have written? And Violet Iris Vacia? What would her story be? She did not know. She had never been able to imagine a future for herself.

Viv secured herself to the trunk with the pack strap and dozed until a faint wash of bird call roused her at dawn and then she tree-travelled her way downslope. The branches flashed with gold-breasted birds and tiny olive ones and the leaves shone with iridescent bugs. The birds and bugs reassured her because it meant this world, whatever it was, might not be too different to her own, except for birdmen and pig-bears of course.

She made good progress, having grown used to judging the strength of the branches she clambered over, and then there were no more trees and Viv found herself staring out over open grasslands.

She could see no blotches that might be pig-bears but they might be crouched in their lairs, waiting for dinner to come on by and she chewed her lip. She could tree-travel along the forest's margin in the hope of finding caves with rifts or until she arrived back at her starting point or she could take to the air and risk another attack. Or she could just sit here. 'Procrastination is just one of my many talents,' she muttered.

The trees provided more cover than the grasslands but the forest looked the same in both directions and after a quick round of eenie-meenie-miny-mo she turned right. The trees provided easy passage but the forest's sweeping curve prevented her seeing far ahead and she had not gone far before she smelled smoke.

Smoke meant people and people meant trouble and she stopped. It might not be *people*, she cautioned, given the uncountable possibilities of the Rynth. *Yeah, sure Vivi. It might be some kinda insect that's mastered the art of fire-making and how to sharpen darts, and cover them in poison, and hit a target as it streaks overhead. In fact, two targets.*

Viv continued cautiously and an encampment came into view. She noticed the horses first because their black coats and rusty manes and tails made them look like something out of a fairy story. They were tethered behind a row of scruffy tents that were scarcely more than tarpaulins slung over ropes. A campfire smouldered nearby and while the encampment looked deserted the horses and fire told Viv the owners were not far.

It looked like some sort of workers' camp and Viv's knuckles whitened on the branch. She had learned from the gangs that men were at their most dangerous in packs but still she lingered. The smell of wood smoke reminded her of the homeliness of the Keeper's cottage and reinforced how alone she was.

It seemed she was doomed to spend the rest of her very long life passing like a wraith along the margins of other people's lives. She half shook her head. No, she told herself firmly, she would spend it getting to know the mother she had believed lost.

Viv turned away from the camp but as she swung herself across to the next tree she heard a cry. It sounded like a birdman but not one that greeted the dawn with joyful choraling or that cawed in triumph or anger. This was a cry wretched with distress and it came from the camp.

Viv climbed higher to get a better view and cautiously parted the leaves. There was a cage beyond the ramshackle row of tents and huddled inside, its red crest dulled with dust, was her attacker. Occasionally it gave a miserable squawk and shuffled its feet but it did not move. Unlike the makeshift tents, the cage was a sophisticated domed contraption of shining metal but the sloping sides meant the birdman could only sit upright in the centre. She could see no food or water inside either, just dusty, trampled grass.

Birds must have clean water, her mother had emphasised when a neighbour had given Viv the budgie chick. *And a nice branch to sit on and most importantly of all, plenty of room to flap their wings. Birds are wild creatures that love to fly.* They had gone to the local tip to scavenge for a cage, straightened its bars and wire-brushed off the rust, and over the following weeks, Viv had watched the hatchling fledge to its adult, powder-blue plumage. It was the blue that had stuck in Viv's mind about her childhood pet, bright on its bloodied wing, amongst the grass.

Viv's anger flared. Not even the bullying, red-crested birdman deserved to be treated so cruelly. It should have butchered while still comatose, not left to suffer! Her keen eyes searched out the cage's lock. It did not look complicated but there was no keyhole which meant the catch must be underneath.

It's too risky Vivi and the thing's not even human, warned Rim's voice. Neither am I, she retorted as she scanned the camp for entry and exit points. Her heart quickened and the familiar mix of dread and excitement pounded through her veins. The sensation had been addictive and at its peak had seen her rob *occupied* houses and challenge gang-leaders for her share of the spoils.

'Vivi's high again,' Rim had sneered, and he had been right, but it had been an intoxication that had danced her along the knife blade between life and death once too often, into the back seat of a car, driven by a druggie who believed he could fly.

Viv could not see whether the tents were occupied but dropped to the ground and set off in a crouching run along the forest's margin. There were no shouts of challenge but the birdman's crest came erect. *Keep your stupid beak shut,* she willed it. The birdman made no sound but it glared at her as if she were to blame for its predicament.

Her new viewpoint revealed the tents held blankets and harness not slumbering bodies and there were no guards either. So far, so good. She darted to the cage, eager to obey the thieves' mantra of *get in quick, get out quicker,* but as she ducked to examine the lock, the birdman's claw scythed through the bars.

Viv jumped back and the birdman slashed again and screeched. 'I'm trying to help you, birdbrain!' she hissed, as she ducked and weaved, intent on the lock.

One of the horses whinnied and an answering whinny came from beyond the forest's curve but as Viv snatched a glance in that direction, the birdman's claw snagged her pack strap. She threw herself backwards but the birdman's claw held fast, pinning her to the cage and then there was the sound of galloping horses.

Chapter 10

Thris woke alone but could not recall whether he had ordered Ky away or Ky had simply left. He hauled himself up and leaned against the tree to steady. He had thought Moth Fold's trees dull on his first visit but now he noticed their similarity to Ezam's darkest umber. They lacked the glis's shifting bronze but like other trees, created a healing somnolence as soft as the resting moths.

He could see the moths' blue and silver daubings among the leaves and memories of their glorious display oozed through him. He was one of the few angels to have witnessed it but he had paid a heavy price. Thris shook his head in savage rebuttal. *He* was responsible for the profound flaws in his makeup, not the moths of Moth Fold, *or* its grubs!

He swung on his pack but the effort left him trembling. The pack was a disguise, for human caste travelled with belongings, but it also contained things the shekinah would need. Early in their transits, she had asked to carry her own things in case they were separated but he had shrugged off the request. Yet another example of his arrogance!

Ash should have abandoned *him* to Beast Fold not the shekinah! He swayed as the full implications of the shekinah's predicament swept over him. He had been so taken up with his failure of the Guideship, he had not considered its effects on her. No wonder Archae Kald had insisted Thris use *whatever means necessary* to bring her back under his protection. It was the only way the Archae could guarantee the shekinah's safety, and her safety was all that mattered.

Thris left the trees and made his way out over the plain. He did not bother to sense for rifts knowing the surest way to locate the shekinah was to use the rift in the putrid cave. He feared its fumes might finally destroy him and Ky complete the Guideship but Ky's dislike of the shekinah risked them both. It also roused troubling memories of Prime-archae Serith's antagonism, so strong, the Prime-archae had wanted the shekinah murdered.

Thris stumbled to a stop. Surely the memory was false? Yet Ky had said something similarly shocking, something about . . . The train of thought fractured and he struggled to rebuild it. Something about the shekinah being *winged*.

The air moved and Ky landed beside him. 'A Shadow remains unseen,' said Thris hoarsely.

'Then shut your eyes,' retorted Ky. Thris said nothing and Ky's expression hardened. 'As I am guessing you intend to revisit that foul, acid-ridden cave where the rift was, I will fly you there to save your strength.'

Thris shook his head. 'A Shadow—' he began.

'Is appointed to ensure the Guideship's success,' finished Ky and gripped Thris's arm. 'You *need* to survive the cave's filth, Thris, to reach Beast Fold to track where the shekinah went next. Your *duty* is to complete the Guideship and the sooner you do so, the sooner we can be away from these stinking places and back in Ezam.' And before Thris could protest, Ky swung him into his arms and took to the air.

Thris struggled not to relinquish his will to his longtime rival but his eyelids drooped and he relaxed against Ky's cool chest, and then there was a bump as Ky came to ground and Thris was enveloped in the most horrendous stench. Ky bound cloth over Thris's mouth and nose but it was not enough and the rents the Principae had left in his healing began to fray.

All sense of Ky disappeared to leave Thris alone in a bitter darkness. It was an ending, he dimly perceived, as different to the glory of the Great Beyond as it was possible to be, and then that awareness disappeared too.

Ky stripped off Thris's clothing as soon as they exited into Sand Fold, cleaned him with sand, and lay naked atop him to gift him healing essence. He hoped their quick passage through the cave had limited the injury to Thris and Ky's confidence soared when Thris's eyes opened and were only slightly darker than normal.

Ky had located the correct cave, predicted where the rift would twin, guided the semi-conscious Thris to Sand Fold, and helped him revive. He had also recognised the shekinah's scent at the rift's juncture and knew she had transited to Sand Fold too, which meant they had no need to risk Beast Fold again. Ky's legs had healed quickly but not his fear of beastman attack.

Ky waited for Thris to laboriously harmonise before outlining the shekinah's movements but Thris insisted on retracing the shekinah's exact route. 'But her scent shows she came *here*,' repeated Ky in frustration. 'There is no need to return to Beast Fold.'

'And her resonance?'

'Her resonance is too muddled to read.'

'Muddled?'

'Too unclear,' muttered Ky as he recalled the uncomfortable conversation with Archae Dejon. *You are familiar with the shekinah's resonance,* the Archae had said, *and with mine and Archae Kald's. You would be wise to consider the nature of each in the task that lies ahead in your role of Shadow.*

And Ky *had* considered it and reached the shocking conclusion Archae Dejon had hinted at. But *if* the shekinah were Archae Dejon's and not Archae Kald's, what did Archae Dejon want him to do about it? And what were the Principaes' intentions? And how did any of it affect his role of Shadow?

Ky did not share his exchange with Archae Dejon. Thris had never countenanced strangeness in the shekinah's resonance and Ky faced the more urgent problem of stopping Thris from risking death a second time. Thris turned back towards the rift and Ky caught his arm. 'Rest first,' he said hurriedly. 'Then you will have the strength to fly from any beastman.'

'I have no time to rest,' he muttered, shrugging him off, and stepped into the rift.

Ky stared after him in horror, his fear of beastmen so great it all but brought him to his knees. His role of Shadow meant he must follow, as did his love for Thris, and he forced himself forward and then gave a howl of dismay. The rift had closed.

Ash trembled on the slab, his turmoil in stark contrast to the serene glow of the walls. Thris and Ky were alone for the first time since leaving Ezam but that was a small thing compared to the risks Ky faced in Sand Fold. Since the shekinah's near-suffocation, Ash had learned that Sand Fold could remain placid for eons, then birth storms that snuffed out all life.

Ash had guided the shekinah to a nearby rift but he feared he lacked the skill to rescue any angel who was not already near a rift, and to add to Ash's worries, Thris had returned to Beast Fold despite knowing the shekinah was no longer there.

Ash's wings fluttered as he wondered whether Thris sought death as human caste sometimes did, but the notion an angel would deliberately snuff out his own life-spark was too shocking to contemplate.

Ash swung himself off the slab and, desperate to learn more of his friends' fate, lay his palms against the wall but the stone remained opaque. His agitation was probably to blame but harmonising was beyond him and he hastened back to the cavern's entrance. The Bokos's scrolls were no use to him now and for all his gentle wisdom, neither was Prime-archae Mirek, and Ash's distracted gaze came to rest on the blood-red pulse of the Red Helixai.

It seemed to summon him and Ash sped away towards it, landed on the lip of a cavern, and gingerly made his way inside. Fire shadows played along the walls and he flattened himself against the stone to avoid sudden flares of flame. He had forgotten the Red Helixai's unsettling strangeness. The stone did not speak to him like the Blue's but nor was it mute and its emanations made him uneasy. He clamped his wings to his back but still imagined them alight and flailed his arms behind him. Part of him clamoured to retreat but the need to reach the mountain's heart was stronger.

Then, just as he thought he could endure no more, he exited into a cavern identical to the Blue's inner cavern in everything except colour. He paused, no, it was not identical. The Blue Helixai's heart was filled with a music made by the wind as it passed through its hollow core but it was silent here.

He went to the slab and peered up. The openings looked the same and despite the odd silence, the urge to stay was strong. Ash perched on the slab. If the Helixai *were* giant steles, as Prime-archae Mirek suggested, they should be besieged by angels, yet he was as lonely here as in the Blue Helixai.

He smiled as he was roused by gusts of warm air that flowed in from the tunnels. The Blue Helixai's harmonies were gloriously familiar and now he was to be gifted the Red's but there were no sweet notes, just a roar as the warm air was replaced by the blast of scorching air. Great gobs of fire followed and Ash leapt onto the slab, intending to fly to safety, but the flames soared to the cavern's roof to form a wall of fire.

Ash whirled, desperate to escape, but the only way out was up. He had no idea if it were even possible to navigate the core of a Helixai. It might split to form a maze of dead ends or narrow to trap him and then the fire would catch him in the dark. He had the wild idea his name was prescient but as the air boiled about him, he did the only thing possible, and leapt upwards.

Chapter 11

Viv fought to free herself from the birdman's claw as the sound of galloping horses drew closer. Her brain screamed at her to abandon the pack but it held Thris's feathers and the horsemen would see it and search for her. The birdman's glare fastened on her hair and in a burst of inspiration, Viv tore out a clump. The pain sent dizzying waves of shock but she tossed the hair into the cage and as the birdman seized it, wrenched herself free and sprinted for the trees.

The nearest one had branches too high to reach as did those nearby and as the first of the horsemen rounded the forest, hooting and cheering, Viv forced her way in between the trunks. She had to angle her shoulders to fit through but her pack jammed and she shucked out of it and scuttled behind some roots.

Her scalp throbbed and the roots gave little cover, being more like ropes fixed high on the trunks, but the horsemen were too busy celebrating to search for an intruder. They hauled their mounts to a stop, churning up dust, and it was moment before Viv noticed they had a second birdman strung between them.

The horses were the odd colours of those tethered and the men were strange too with the same rusty-coloured hair as the horses' manes and tails, light olive skin, and solid, muscular builds. They looked eerily similar and Viv guessed she noticed it because Australia's cultural mix made everyone look different.

The men had crowded around the birdman and Viv flinched as a knife flashed but as they bundled it into the cage, she realised they had cut its bonds. The birdman staggered about the cramped enclosure, its plight worsened by the red-crested birdman slashing at it whenever it lurched too close.

A bully to the last, thought Viv sourly, *and* moronic. No one ever beat an enemy by fighting alone, even the dumbest gang member knew that. Some upstart hustler and his hangers-on would muscle in on Rim's territory and the band would unite, all arguments forgotten, or the cops would turn up and suddenly old foes were best buds, watching each other's backs.

It was getting dark but the men did not rebuild the fire or prepare food but drew off to one side. Viv could not see what was going on but she could hear arguing and the men charged with looking after the horses clearly resented being excluded. They tossed the harness in a heap and dragged water buckets near the tether rope but did not bother to rub the horses down.

Viv had once had a friend who owned a pony and they had spent hours grooming it, riding it, and cleaning its harness. Her friend's mum had set treats on the kitchen table for them and Viv had not only learned about horses, but about houses that were free from threat, and then her friend had shifted away.

The men's argument ceased and coins were slapped down, then they spat, obviously sealing a deal but what kind of deal? Maybe one lot had sold the birdman to the other lot *or* its meat, but surely the deal did not need them all to be involved?

The men moved off towards the tents, and kegs were rolled out, and they started to drink. Viv grimaced. The only thing worse than a pack of men was a pack of *drunken* men. The mesh of tree roots prevented a quick escape and she decided to wait for darkness to slip away. It meant abandoning the birdmen but she had no choice.

Viv's legs ached from crouching and she eased her backside onto the ground. At least the second birdman had recovered from whatever had drugged it and now sat as miserably as the first, in fact, more miserably given it was forced to hunch under the cage's sloping roof.

The first stars woke and, as one of the men opened the cage door and tossed something inside, Viv realised three things: the lock was released by twisting clockwise; the cage was a giant cock-fighting ring; and the men's argument had been over sorting the odds. Viv had no idea what was tossed into the cage but it was shiny, and that was enough.

Shouting began but Viv moved away through the roots. They were too dense to slide through and she had to clamber over the top but the men were so absorbed in the fight she could have waltzed along the forest's margin unnoticed.

As soon as she could, she swung herself into a tree and climbed to its crown. She felt safer off the ground but its height gave her a good view of the carnage in the cage. The red-crested birdman was the bigger and the more aggressive of the two but the fight dragged on, the smaller birdman's wing sliced, and its body bloodied from its clashes with the cage.

The men roared their appreciation but Viv could scarcely bear to watch. 'For God's sake, give-up,' she muttered and then realised the curved sides of the cage prevented it signaling submission. And it was deliberate; the men *intended* this to be a fight to the death.

'You cruel bastards,' she breathed and swung herself back down the tree.

The star-sheen gave enough light to see *and* be seen and she hoped to God the men kept their eyes on the show. She darted along the back of the tents but while the fire still smoked, there were no red coals *or* fuel. Shit! She should have brought a dry branch from the trees. She gazed about wildly, saw a jumble of rope, and grabbed an end.

Viv rarely experienced prescience but she knew she was being watched and froze. Run or fly, Viv? Make up your bloody mind! Her heart pounded and she turned, expecting heavy hands to descend on her, but there was nothing. It was the horses that watched her, ears pricked, faces turned in unison.

A whicker ran along the line and the hair on Viv's neck stirred. Horses were intelligent but not *that* intelligent. She was convinced they exchanged information about her but whether they passed it onto their riders was the real question and she sure as hell was not hanging about to find out.

The men's shouts had turned to jeers which told her the fight was almost over and Viv dragged the end of the rope to the fire. She wanted a nice little tent fire as a distraction while she freed the birdmen and went on her way. The rope stank of rancid fat which she hoped would help it burn but as fire raced back along its length, Viv had an instant to realise whatever soaked it was highly flammable, and then the world exploded.

Chapter 12

The blast threw Viv backwards and she landed with a thump that knocked the air from her lungs, then choking black smoke billowed and the ground vibrated as the horses broke their tethers and galloped away. She felt the thud of human feet too, scrambled up and flung herself into the nearest tent as men rushed past, then cautiously peered out.

The second birdman looked close to death and she dashed to the cage and, with a flick of her wrist, threw open the door. 'Out,' she hissed, but the birdmen were intent on whatever they had fought over. 'Get out!' she shrieked but they did not move. They would follow the object but retrieving it meant risking being attacked or trapped.

'Rim *was* right, I *am* mad,' she muttered, as she ducked inside and snatched up the object. She had an instant to see it was a bracelet and then the red-crested birdman lunged, there was a shout, and the cage door slammed shut. Viv had once been cornered by a member of a rival gang whose hatred of Rim was exceeded only by his brutality, and a moment of paralysing fear had been followed by an adrenaline rush that had left the man with broken teeth and her safely away.

The same desperate power jolted her now and she threw herself under the birdman's claw, held the bracelet aloft until its eyes fastened on it, then appeared to hurl it from the cage. In truth she shoved it under her sleeve but the birdman launched in the same direction, slammed into the bars, and fell back stunned.

Viv reached through the cage and twisted the lock but nothing happened. *Shit! Shit! Shit!* One of the men

66

was running back and then pain seared her arm as the birdman's claw sliced home. She twisted the lock in the opposite direction, the door opened, and she half fell out and ran.

The star-sheen was as bright as a full moon and Viv knew the man pursued her. She would have added him to the list of frustrated arseholes she had left in her wake had she not been injured, but her shirt was sodden with blood and she was already light-headed. There was a high-pitched whistle and she snatched a glance over her shoulder. The man had stopped but any hope he had given up was short-lived. A blotch appeared behind him, coming fast. It was a horse and in one smooth motion, the man had vaulted on its back and had closed half the distance between them before she had the wits to move.

The man cut between her and the trees to block any chance of escape and while she still had the element surprise, she was loath to reveal her wings, visions of witch-burnings never far away. Anger surged and she swung around to face him. She did not think he would kill her, at least not before he and his mates had some fun, but he failed to slow and she wondered whether he would run her down after all.

His eyes bored into hers, surprisingly dark given his rusty-coloured hair and then, without slowing, he grabbed her arm and wrenched her off the ground. He probably intended to throw her over the front of his horse but he had grabbed her wounded arm which was greasy with blood and his hand slipped.

The horse danced sideways as he struggled to hold her and Viv dangled limply, in too much pain to fight, and then she heard a harsh grunting. God in heaven! A pig-bear! The horse heard it too and gave a terrified whinny. The man barked an order, but the horse was beyond obedience and the man lost his grip on Viv completely. She crumpled to the ground and lay still, knowing if the pig-bear went for her, she was a goner, but it was intent on the horse.

Maybe her blood smeared along the horse's side attracted it, or maybe horses and pig-bears were natural enemies. The man clipped out orders but she smelled the horse's sweat and then the pig-bear charged. The star-sheen glanced off its tusks and Viv thought the horse's legs would be slashed but at the last moment the man shouted a command and the horse jumped sideways. Like a cat, thought Viv in astonishment.

The pig-bear's momentum carried it past and it turned, squealing in fury. The man wrenched the horse around to face it and shot a glance at Viv. He did not want to lose his prize but he had no weapons to fight the pig-bear and the horse fought *him*.

Bad luck, arsehole, thought Viv, as she tensed for the pig-bear's next assault. The result of its charge was the same but as soon as it passed, Viv launched from the grass, pumped her good arm to build momentum, and fled towards the trees. She was so light-headed she barely felt her feet hit the ground but there was no sound of pursuit. The man had to turn his back on the pig-bear to give chase and the risk was too great.

The pig-bear might have switched its attention to her too but Viv had chosen her moment well, no more than a fleeing shadow in contrast to the sweating, snorting, blood-smelling lump of flesh the horse presented.

Citrus fumed from her skin as she threw herself into the roots and scrambled along under them as fast as her wounded arm allowed. She head-butted some and snagged her pack on others; the roots an effective a cage as the birdmen's metal one. She finally found a gap and squeezed up through to lay trembling on their knobby surface.

She needed to wash her arm and bind it with something clean; she needed to rest to help it heal; she needed Thris. Tears squeezed from under her lids and she drew a choking breath. *What? No white knight to the rescue, Vivi? Looks like ya gunna have to help herself.*

'Get stuffed, Rim,' she croaked and cranked herself up, only to hit her head on a branch above. 'About time my luck changed,' she muttered, relieved to have branch she could reach. Her legs were like jelly and climbing one-handed was a nightmare but she needed to find somewhere beyond the reach of pig-bears and men.

When she could climb no further, she laboriously secured herself to the trunk with the pack strap and shrugged her wounded arm free from of her sleeve. A ragged rent ran from shoulder to elbow and Viv groaned and rested her head back against the bole.

Starlight limned the leaves and then they rustled as wings stirred the glittering air. 'Thris,' she whispered in wonder, as a luminous form alighted on the branch in front of her, but it was a birdman.

Chapter 13

Roaith en-Leferen ruffled his feathers as he surveyed the Valen. It was still now, its head having flopped to one side but it had moved as he had come to his roost and so had yet to join the Quiet Ones. Roaith chittered softly as seed memories joined shell memories and reconfigured. This Valen had been at the Circle of Silence, had fled the morrog, had shared his *nyth*, and then passed out of the Song.

But Garian's cawings had woven a new Song and inserted seed memories into the swirl of shell memories; seed memories that were jagged with blood and confinement, and he had sent Roaith, with his seed memories of the Valen, in search of it, here at the Song's very edge.

The trees smelled of Valen, of their stealing and slaying, for while they could not penetrate the Leferen, their poisons pervaded its margins, borne on darts as lethal as the morrog. Yet *this* Valen had travelled the trees *and* the sky *and* it had freed Garian.

The Valen smelled of blood and Roaith was reminded of the awful emptiness of the highest roost. Garian's mate-pair tended him in his nyth like an egg-wet chick, and Roaith gathered himself and sprang to land on the trunk above the Valen's head. He anchored himself there with his claws, pressed his soles against the bark, and listened.

The kirrik was too remote from the Song to be a regular feeding-tree and unfamiliar with its sweet flows, he hauled himself higher and pressed his soles against the bark again, this time to be rewarded with a rhythmic thrum. Spreading his feet for balance, he released one claw, made a surgical incision in the bark, then slid his slender tongue into the wound and drew the liquid deep into his craw.

Kirrik were abundant in the Rookery but no two flows were the same. This one was sweeter than Roaith preferred but he did not harvest it for himself. When his craw was full he swung himself back down to the Valen. The Valen's hair shone like flame in the star-sheen and for a moment Roaith forgot everything but its brightness, then the swirl of seed memories jelled and he saw the Valen's need again.

A trill throbbed from his throat and he arched, slid his tongue deep into the Valen's mouth, and disgorged the sweet liquid. When his craw was empty he settled back to his roost and as the night deepened and the air cooled, enclosed the Valen in the shelter of his wings. The Valen did not stir again but Roaith sensed its growing ease and when he knew it slept, his own eyes closed too.

Viv woke to the chill of dawn, fumbled her jacket from her pack, pulled it over her, and went back to sleep. The light was riper the next time she woke, this time roused by thirst. She found Thris's water bottle and drank. The water tasted sweet, as if Thris had added ambrosia. She hoped he had. It would help heal her aching arm.

At least there was no sign of the birdman from last night and Viv wondered why it had not finished her off and it might have, had it seen the nice shiny bracelet she wore. She held her wrist to the light. The bracelet was heavy enough to be solid silver and beautifully etched with a pattern of swirling waves. It looked valuable and she guessed the men intended to retrieve it after the fight.

Thris's warning about transference between folds rang in her ears and she decided bury it before she transited.

It would prevent the birdmen fighting if nothing else, but first there was the little matter of finding a rift. Taking to the air risked attack from the dart-throwers and mates of the red-crested birdman, and staying on the ground risked attack from the man on the horse and *his* mates. It also risked pig-bears but her best chance of finding a rift was on the ground.

Viv's breath sifted between her teeth. The men might have gone by now *or* be sneaking about with their dart guns. And if they *had* gone, where had they gone to? The last thing she wanted was to stumble on a stinking nest of them. Of course, the third possibility was they were in the trees searching for *her*. The man on the horse had got a good look at her and she wondered how visible she had been when chased by the red-crested bully in the air. The men might already know they had a winged-witch in their midst.

Viv stared at the surrounding leaves uneasily. The sooner she quit this fold the better! She would wait for dark then fly as high and far as possible to some new place and search for a rift there. She should be safe in the trees until then or at least safer than on the ground.

Being light meant she could climb higher into the brittle trees than any pursuer *except* the birdmen. Maybe they shared her *hollow bones*, she thought dourly. It was a quip some nurse had once made. Viv's lightness had caused consternation among the medical profession, though not enough for them to investigate, but what if they had?

They probably would have come up with a name for her condition related to some genetic disorder. *Bonus hollowus.* They would have been right too, except the name should have been *bonus angelicus*. The birdmen flew so they must be light as well and then, as if summoned by her thoughts, a birdman dropped through the canopy.

Viv clutched the pack like a shield but the birdman simply settled on the branch, cocked its head, and chittered. It looked like the same one whose nest she had shared but it was hard to be sure and then, without warning, its sinuous tongue flicked towards her.

Viv instinctively swatted it away and the birdman chittered again, higher this time. It had not acted like this before, thought Viv, as she fended off its tongue a second time. The birdman hopped from foot to foot, head cocked. It appeared to be thinking and Viv reminded herself that slow did not necessarily mean stupid, a distinction Rim had discovered when a *dumb as dog-shit* gang member he had abused for weeks suddenly broke his nose.

Viv started as the birdman flapped its wings, rose off the branch and before she could dodge, delivered a stream of vomit into the wound on her arm. She gasped in horror at the thought of the infection-seething contents of the birdman's stomach, but the pale gold liquid smelled faintly of the trees and as it dripped from the wound, it took with it dirt she had collected in her mad scramble through the roots.

The birdman chittered again, a satisfied chitter this time, Viv thought, and disappeared through the foliage. It reappeared, looked at Viv, then repeated the maneuver. 'Not this time, my friend,' said Viv softly. The word *friend* sounded strange in her ears for she used the word so rarely. The birdman repeated the trick a third time and then she heard the scythe of wings. 'Stay safe,' she whispered, unable to bear the thought of it ending its days in a blood-spattered cage.

Viv used the daylight hours to review what she knew of rifts, which was not much, and she hoped she had overlooked something that would help her find her mother. Thris had said the gathering of birds and the dead often signaled rifts and that rifts were more common in caves. It was why he had searched the caves in Moth Fold; and the rift from Moth Fold had been in a cave and the rift to Hearth Fold opened in an underground cavern. Then again, the rifts to Moth Fold, from the cat creature's fold, to and from the sand-filled fold, and the rift here, wherever here was, had been in the open.

Viv sighed. Finding a rift was only the start of her problems. She needed one that took her to her mother. Thris had intended to track Viv's mother through scent and resonance which were sort of like fingerprints but Viv did not have the skill to recognise such things although she could tell the difference between Thris, Ky and Ash's fragrances. They all smelled sweet but Ash was like roses, Ky like jasmine, and Thris like honeysuckle or he *had* been.

She took a shaky breath. He's dead, Viv, accept it. There's still a chance . . . She could almost hear Rim's derisive laughter. *Seen any pigs flappin' past lately, Vivi? Any clean, honest druggies?*

She pushed the curls from her eyes. This was why people went to morgues, searched burned houses, begged murderers to tell them of that place in the bush, dam, murky river where their loved ones lay. Humans needed *proof* there would be no coming home but even that was not enough for her. She had *seen* Thris ripped apart by the cat creature, carried his broken feathers in her pack, and wore the single undamaged one over her heart, but stubborn, bloody-minded hope had taken up residence in her head and like a stinking squatter, it refused to move on.

Chapter 14

By the time the stars sent their silvery light through the leaves, Viv had fastened her pack to her waist and fashioned her shirt into halter-neck. She was pleased with the effect. Tying the shirt sleeves around her neck, crossing its tails low on her back, and knotting them in front meant she no longer had to fly half naked.

The gash on her arm was part healed but still hampered her tree-travel and she was relieved when the forest gave way to grasslands. They stretched away like a pale sea in the starlight and Viv unbedded her wings and powered away, the rush of cool air and starfalls of light so exhilarating she forgot her fear of being seen. The air seemed to chime with notes as clear as bells and she hovered spellbound.

'Are you here, Thris?' she whispered to the sky. 'Is this what you wanted?' The stars blurred and she blinked hard. 'Are you happy now?'

She turned her gaze earthwards but saw nothing but darkness. No campfires, no streetlights, no headlights of moving cars. She had no idea where the birdmen's captors came from but it was likely to be nearer rather than further away, and she turned to her left and when she had flown a considerable distance, descended in a long, slow, glide.

Grasslands emerged first, followed by scattered trees, and shadowy clefts. It was an odd landscape. She had seen an immense peak when chased by the birdmen and now she saw the forest and grasslands sat about the peak's shoulders in even bands, and that the clefts were the heads of deep valleys that ran away from the peak like the spokes of a wheel.

She was reminded of Ezam's symmetry and wondered whether there were angels here too. The men were certainly not angelic, but there might be castes that carried angelic blood, that lived longer, that her mother had made a home with. The odds were probably worse than winning the lottery but she needed *something* to hold on to.

She smelled smoke again and angled up sharply as blotches of fire appeared. They were too big for campfires and she wondered if they were bushfires. She swerved to her left, wanting to leave any trace of humans behind, and passed over more valleys and rugged spurs and then, as weariness set in, descended into a valley and hovered.

Her wings made soft swishes in the mist and the moist air held the bright scent of peppermint. There was the rush of water too. Cliffs loomed from the darkness to either side, holding the promise of rifts, and she came to earth. It was very quiet. Trees glimmered like shadowy sentinels and she remained poised, her senses trained on her surroundings, her wings primed for take-off.

An owl called, making her jump, and she had an eerie feeling she had strayed back home. Common sense told her it was impossible and that any fold that held men and horses, could hold owls too. Even so, the land's resemblance to the Ranges near her childhood home was unsettling.

She shivered, cold now she had stopped moving, bedded her wings and pulled on her jacket, leaving it unfastened. The mist made it hard to see anything but it meant others would find it hard to see her too. Her belly rumbled and she took off the pack. Fear and hurt always made her hungry but as she searched for food, her fingers brushed Thris's bloodied feathers and she recoiled, slung the pack back over her shoulder, and set off in search of the water.

The stream was wedged between rocky banks and she knelt on the dewy stones and washed her hands. It was easy to wash away Thris's blood but her last sight of him was burned into her brain.

She took a long cool drink from the water and sleeved her mouth as she stared at the opposite bank. It was a lot higher and thick with ferns that glistened with moisture. The stream was full of rounded boulders and those that edged the stream mantled with emerald moss. She could have been happy here had Thris been with her. *Still believe in fairy stories, do ya, Vivi? How sweet.*

Viv sighed and set off up the slope behind her. Just put one foot in front of the other, she told herself. Get through this night and then get through tomorrow, and then tomorrow night. Her heart leapt as a blotch of darkness above heralded a cave and she struggled up to it. There were no smells of animals such as pig-bears and she tried not to think of spiders as she slipped inside. It was warmer in the cave and using the pack as a pillow, she curled up on the floor and tried to sleep.

Ash panted in terror as he powered up through the utter darkness of the Red Helixai's core. Fire seemed forever on the brink of overtaking him but he was guided by something other than sight. His strength gave way to a slough of citrus and then to a state of otherness. He was outside time, flesh and feathers stripped away to reveal a crystal of consciousness that hurtled ever upwards. He burst from the Helixai's crown and floated, as light as gossamer on the updraft of hot air, then gently drifted back to earth to settle in a shining, motionless heap.

The first thing Ash noticed when he roused were his wings folded across him in perfect symmetry and odd though their positioning was, it was their hue that riveted him. Their lower portions were completely white. He felt no rush of horror at the change, which was strange, and there was no soreness from his exertions. He felt normal, well, not normal exactly, but at peace.

In the past such an ordeal would have sent him flapping panic-stricken to Prime-archae Mirek, and he must inform the Prime-archae of what had occurred, yet he felt no urgency. His time in the Red Helixai's fire-filled core had changed him as profoundly as the Blue Helixai's exquisite music, and he needed time to understand his new state.

He sat next to the vent which, like so much in Ezam, was circular in shape. The Dendrinai; the rings of the Hollow Hills and Thorny Mountains; the four circular lakes equi-distant from the four Helixai, all held their own symmetry and he considered what else in Ezam shared the same quality. He had no idea how many steles there were or members of the Host, only that new Dane blinked into being when Archae transcended and Principae passed into the Great Beyond, although they did so from Crystal Fold not Ezam.

Ash faltered as he realised it contradicted the accepted wisdom that folds functioned independently. Perhaps the angelic nature of Ezam and Crystal Folds made them the exception but Erath Fold was angelic too, and he wondered uneasily whether his *accidental* transit there had not been accidental at all.

Next he considered his *visions* of other folds. He had witnessed Thris's attack on the shekinah and the beastman's attack on Thris as if in a dream but he had actually *intruded* into Sand Fold to guide the shekinah to safety.

He stared down at the lands below and for the first time saw their strangeness as an outsider might. The sensation was disturbing and he launched from the peak into a long slow glide, aware of steles amongst the glis but continuing until he slid through the canopy near the Bokos's door. The Bokos seemed light inside after the utter darkness of the Red Helixai's core and he had no difficulty navigating to Prime-archae Mirek's usual workplace but it was Prime-archae Serith who pored over scrolls in the window's light.

He looked up before Ash could retreat and Ash bowed and palmed but the Prime-archae's attention was fixed on Ash's shoulders and Ash realised in mortification he had forgotten to bed his wings. 'I . . . I am seeking Prime-archae Mirek,' he said.

'Yes,' said Serith.

'Can you tell me—' began Ash.

'I warned Mirek of this,' said Serith abruptly, making Ash's heart thud. 'The darkness was terrible,' he muttered, his face like a skin-clad skull. 'Was it the Black Obsidian Stele?'

'I visited the Red Helixai. It—'

'I had not thought of that,' murmured Serith. 'There is so much to be learned. So much.' He roused. 'I will inform Prime-archae Mirek of your arrival,' he said and disappeared into the gloom.

Ash was still struggling to make sense of Prime-archae Serith's words when Prime-archae Mirek appeared and ordered him to turn. Ash did so reluctantly and heard the Prime-archae's intake of breath. 'Tell me everything,' the Prime-archae said.

Chapter 15

Serith stepped from the Bokos's dark stone doorway and set off through the glis, intent on resting his mind in the Dendrinai's beauty. As a Dane, he had been enthralled by the glis and its animal caste but had forgotten them when he discovered the Bokos, *until* the Black Obsidian Stele's intrusion.

His steps faltered and he reminded himself, *yet again*, that all things in Ezam were set there by the Great Beyond to guide the Host, not to harm them. He stopped under a stand of glis, heavy with gold and orange blooms and crowded with feeding lacewings, and considered their jeweled wings then thought of Ashdane's wings and the shekinah's. He still believed the shekinah was perilous but the Black Obsidian Stele had taught him that *all* things in Ezam were perilous, including him.

A blue-robed angel approached but even the possibility it was Archae Kald failed to disturb Serith. The Black Obsidian Stele had also taught him the true meaning of fear. The Archae turned out to be Dejon and Serith bowed and palmed. 'Prime-archae Serith, I am pleased to see you abroad once more,' said Dejon pleasantly.

'I thank you, Archae.'

'You have resumed your studies?' Serith nodded. 'Some subject other than daimon, I presume?' said Dejon lightly.

'Indeed no, Archae,' said Serith. 'I have even more reason to investigate their nature now.'

'More reason?'

'Your protégé reports Archae Kald's shekinah is winged. Given human caste elements subsume angelic ones, such a phenomenon is a mystery. The most likely explanation

81

is that at least one of the shekinah's parents was daimon. As Archae Kald is most certainly angel caste, it must be the shekinah's mother. The Tome mentions no instances of daimon birthing daimon but countless numbers of the Bokos's scrolls remain unsearched.'

'You are amongst the most learned of the Host,' said Dejon, his gaze on the lacewings. 'Do *you* believe such an explanation is likely?'

'The possibilities of the Rynth are endless,' said Serith, 'but no, I do not believe the explanation is likely.' Dejon looked at him startled, but Serith continued before he could speak. 'I do not believe even that would create a caste with sufficient angel essence to manifest wings. Human caste elements are simply too dense.'

'Then how do you account for a winged daimon?'

'I do not,' said Serith with a smile. 'Which is why I continue my studies.'

'I understand the blue angel Ashdane is mentored by Prime-archae Mirek,' said Dejon, his gaze on the lacewings again.

'Ashdane has no mentor,' said Serith. 'He seeks advice from the Prime-archae and the Prime-archae gifts it as a friend. He is with the Prime-archae now at the Bokos.' Dejon strode away through the glis and Serith smiled gently and wandered on.

Mirek was considering Ash's remarkable tale when Archae Dejon appeared around the bookcases. Mirek bowed and palmed but rued having had no time to counsel Ashdane. He just hoped the blue angel had the wits to keep his wings close to his back. Dejon wasted no time on pleasantries simply ordered Ashdane to tell him of any further dreams he had experienced.

Ashdane delivered a briefer version of what he told Mirek but it was soon clear Dejon was only interested in the Shadow and Guide's separation. 'Can you communicate with those you observe in these *dreams*, Ashdane?' he demanded.

'I have yet to attempt to, Archae.'

'You will attempt to now. You will go to the Blue Helixai or wherever succors these *dreams* and instruct Kydane to rejoin the Guide immediately. You will make it clear these are my express orders. Is that understood, Ashdane?'

'Yes Archae.'

'And when you have done so, you will report to me at the Halls.'

The Archae swept out and Mirek poured two goblets of ambrosia and handed one to Ashdane. 'As newer angels, Archae Dejon shared a *competitive spirit* with Arche Kald,' he said carefully. 'Such a *spirit* would prefer Kydane to be Guide, rather than Thrisdane. *I* would prefer to see *both* Dane safely back in Ezam and I suspect you would too, Ashdane.'

'Yes, Prime-archae.'

The blue angel was surprisingly calm, given the Archae's visit, and Mirek looked at him closely. 'You have changed, Ashdane, and I do not mean just your wings.'

'I feel it also, Prime-archae.'

'What will you do?'

'As the Archae commands,' replied Ash in surprise. 'I cannot follow Thris and Ky, at least at this time. The rifts are closed to me.' He gave a small shrug. 'Perhaps you were right to suggest I can better aid Ky and Thris from

Ezam.' He faltered. 'I . . . I did not mean to question your judgement, Prime-archae.'

'I did not interpret it so,' Mirek reassured him. 'I do not claim perfection, Ashdane, but I ask that when you make your way to the Halls to report to Archae Dejon, you make your way past here first.'

'Of course, Prime-archae,' said Ash, and bowed.

Thris stumbled from the rift into Beast Fold, wrenched off his pack, and beat his wings. This was the place of his final disintegration, the end of journey that had begun with his arrival in Ezam fatally flawed. He half expected a beastman to bound from the jungle to finish him off but the only sound was flowing water and for want of something better to do, he set off in its direction.

The stream was small and he followed it to where it cascaded into to a clear pool and, wanting to rid himself of Moth Fold's taint, stripped off and dived in. He powered deeper and deeper into its depths then relaxed his body and let the water bring him back to the surface.

Silvery bubbles swirled around him like miniature folds but then someone called him and he swiveled in surprise. 'Ky?' He peered up but the sky was empty. 'Ky?' he repeated more loudly.

Ky.

The voice came again and Thris floundered as understanding dawned the voice was in his head. 'Ash? What is it?' he whispered. 'What is it you want?'

Sand Fold.

'You want me to go back to Sand Fold, Ash? Is that what you want?' Every nerve tingled. Ash had somehow managed to speak to him from Ezam. *Ky* and then *Sand*

Fold. Thris's heart thundered. 'Ash? Is Ky in need?' The silence was ominous and Thris swam hurriedly to shore, threw on his clothes, and hastened back to the rift. It was open but he was still enclosed by its iridescent swirl when he heard howling. For a horrible moment he feared he had transited to Redice Fold and then he was thrown out into a squalling storm of sand.

There was no boundary between earth and sky just a demonic howling and grit that threatened to flay him alive. He wrapped his shirt around his face but could still barely breathe and there was no sign of Ky. Thris feared he would end his life here but Ash would not have sent him to his death.

Turn.

The word sounded in his head and he turned and had taken half a dozen steps when he stumbled over something buried in the sand and needed no instructions on what to do next. He hauled Ky over his shoulder and devoted every shred of strength to finding the rift.

Sand swallowed the air and Thris might have let it swallow him had it not been for Ky. He struggled on and when he could endure no more, stumbled into a blessed place of nothingness. He managed to remain upright until the rift gave way to solid ground and then collapsed onto the tussocky grass. Ky was sent sprawling and the impact jolted him awake. He coughed and retched while Thris lay beside him and gasped for breath.

Ky's coughing gave way to sobs and Thris gathered him close. He was reluctant to offer Ky his own *flawed* essence but when Ky's distress showed no signs of easing, Thris exhaled over him and Ky fell into an exhausted sleep. And only then did Thris have time to take in his surroundings.

Chapter 16

They were in the fold's dark cycle, assuming it had a *light* cycle, and a Moonsun-like mist made it hard to see anything at all. From what he *could* see, they were in a steep-sided valley, like those in Moonsun and Hearth Folds, and the resemblance to these folds was strengthened by the spicy scent of a plant caste.

New folds held new dangers but it was quiet and his thoughts went to Ash's extraordinary ability to communicate across the Rynth. Nor was it Ash's only achievement. Ash had guided Thris to safety from the Blue Helixai's tunnels, retrieved him after the beastman's attack, and used sweet music to aid his recovery.

Ash's feats had not gone unnoticed by the Principae either. Thris had been too damaged to recognise the significance of Ash's snowy plumage in Haven but he recognised it now. When he had set out with the shekinah, he had thought he had left Ash and Ky behind, and his triumphal return would see him elevated to Quin-archae while they remained Dane. He had even believed it after Ky became Shadow, but now he saw Ash had left them both behind.

Ky sat up, his eyes dark with fear. 'I thought I would die,' he croaked. 'The sand . . . and the terrible shrieking . . .' Tears slid down his face. 'I am not journeying alone, Thris. I am staying with you.'

'The Shadow remains separate,' said Thris gently.

'No!' Ky caught Thris's hand. 'My task is to ensure the Guideship is completed. This time . . .' he swallowed convulsively, 'this time you aided me, but in Moth Fold, I aided *you*. We *need* to stay together.'

Thris disengaged his hand and rose. 'I am bound to obey Archae Kald.'

'Does he order you to journey alone?' demanded Ky, scrambling to his feet.

'No.'

'My mentor's orders do not stop me from helping you either.'

Thris looked at him blankly. He had left Ezam knowing he would relinquish his life to ensure Ky completed the Guideship *and* ascended but until this moment, the understanding had occupied a different part of his brain to his mentor's orders to keep the shekinah close. Thris's thoughts were as scattered as leaves in a wind and he swayed as he fought to impose order on them.

Ky gripped his arm. 'Your healing is not complete, Thris. The Guideship will fail *unless* we work together.'

Thris shivered, chill suddenly. 'We need to find shelter for the night,' he said. 'Come.'

Ash panted as the vision slipped away. It had taken him countless cycles to hone his skills enough to reunite Thris and Ky but Archae Dejon might still be angered by Ky's determination to aid Thris. Whatever the case, he could do no more, too exhausted even to search for ambrosia.

Music dusted down from the Helixai's core and Ash turned his leaden head in time to see glittering motes settle on his skin. He closed his eyes in dread and when he opened them again, his skin looked normal and his weariness had gone.

Ash did not question the change just hastened back to the cavern's mouth. The Red Helixai still burned with rubescent fire and the White and Green glowed too. Ash sensed he would journey within them all before his time in Ezam ended but the time was not now.

He flew to the Bokos to report his achievement to Prime-archae Mirek, then onto the Halls. Archae Dejon seemed satisfied his protégé was back with the Guide and reiterated his orders to report any further *dreams* to him. Ash hastened back into the glis to relieve the discomfort of his bedded wings and had just stretched them to their fullest breadth when Archae Kald stepped from the glis. Ash hastily bowed and palmed but Kald remained rooted to the spot.

A Dane with snowy wings! Kald's shock was profound but momentary. Ashdane kept company with his own protégé *and* with Dejon's. He also had a mentor-like relationship with a lesser Archae who claimed Ashdane *dreamed* the Guideship had gone amiss and then Kald had discovered *it had*!

Kald's breath seethed in and out as he recognised a previously unsuspected pattern of interference in his affairs. Dejon sought to claim *his* shekinah and Dejon's protégé Shadowed *his* protégé. And now Ashdane, who kept company with both, purported to dream of the two. No doubt he shared his fancies with the lesser Archae, who in turn shared them with Dejon, the very Archae, Kald guessed, from whom the blue angel had just come.

'You have been in discussion with Archae Dejon?' he demanded. The Dane nodded. 'Of what did you speak?' Ashdane had no *formal* mentor so Kald could question him with impunity.

'Archae Dejon asked me to report Thris and Ky's experiences in the folds.'

'And what *are* their experiences in the folds?' asked Kald sarcastically.

'Ky came close to death in Sand Fold but I warned Thris to go back for him. They are together now and safe, but yet to find the shekinah.'

Kald was speechless. Not only did the Dane claim to see into other folds but to *communicate* with them too! *And* he passed on news of *his* protégé to Dejon! The Dane's impudence was infuriating but Kald dare not vent his anger on an angel so obviously blessed by the Principae.

Kald's thwarted want to punish pushed him to the edge of disjoint and he set off through the glis, thrusting vines from his path and not slowing even when he reached the Bokos. He strode between the bookcases, swept around a turn, and collided with an angel.

Serith was so changed Kald took a moment to recognise him but he noted the lesser angel's slowness to bow and palm. 'I seek Prime-archae Mirek,' snapped Kald, but Serith's face remained maddeningly blank.

'You are the Guide's mentor and the shekinah's father,' said Serith eventually. 'The Guide has yet to find her.'

'*You* also purport to know what happens in other folds?' sneered Kald. 'It seems half the Host lay claim to such a faculty.'

'Ezam has but one blue angel,' the lesser angel droned. 'So many hues but only one blue. Perhaps Ezam is too fragile to bear more than one at any given time.'

'Why should a *blue* angel be more important than another colour?' demanded Kald.

'That I do not know, Archae,' said Serith, seeming to focus on him for the first time. 'I have wondered whether it is but one element in a rare but potent combination. The scrolls speak of Senquar-archae, who was also blue and blessed with early ascension. Senquar-archae appeared in

Ezam with two others but the scrolls do not speak of a winged daimon. My studies remain—'

Kald's hand fastened on his arm. '*Winged* daimon?'

'An interesting anomaly, is it not?' asked Serith with a gentle smile. 'For a daimon to be winged, it must—'

'Ashdane claims the daimon is winged?' cut in Kald hoarsely.

'It was Kydane who reported it.'

The *Dane* the Principae had appointed as Shadow! The *Dane* Dejon would have as Guide! Kald's disjoint was complete and so alien he was barely aware of having left the Bokos or of how he reached his rooms. He gulped down several goblets of ambrosia, tore off his robes, and harmonised. Only then could he impose order on his thoughts and when he did, his rigor was brutal.

He replenished his supply of ambrosia many times and harmonised again but each fact led inexorably to a single catastrophic conclusion. He must visit Dejon, for the matter concerned them both, but he was determined to resolve it in his favour. The shekinah *was* his and having *his* protégé as her Guide strengthened his claim.

Thrisdane must return her to Ezam immediately, for a winged daimon was closer to angel caste than human caste, and must be placed among the Iahhel of Erath Fold. The fold was closed to the Host so the Principae must auspice her delivery there *if* they chose, or elsewhere *if* Erath Fold rejected her. In either case, having fully and appropriately discharged his responsibilities, she would no longer be his concern.

The only risk to his transcendence would be Thrisdane's failure to return the shekinah to Ezam but presuming Ashdane had the skills he claimed, Kald's orders should be quickly conveyed, the shekinah promptly returned, and the whole unfortunate episode brought to a swift conclusion.

Kald steepled his fingers as he searched for something he might have overlooked. His plan ensured his own behaviour remained exemplary but not his protégé's. Seducing a near-Iahhel would condemn the Dane to the Host's lowest rank for eons and the taint deny him the aid of a mentor for eternity.

Kald shrugged and considered Dejon. The Archae had attempted to steal Kald's transcendence by claiming the shekinah as his own and had worked against Kald since. That, pledged Kald with an icy smile, was about to end.

Chapter 17

V iv was relieved when dawn's cool light slid into the cave. Since her angel traits had emerged, she could only sleep when exhausted or injured and apart from letting her crappy memories roam free, the dark gave her too much time to stew on her predicament.

Her jacket was filthy and she wondered just how much dirtier and ragged she would be before she found her mother. *Hark! Hark! The dogs do bark, the beggars are coming to town.* The nursery rhyme popped uninvited into her head and her eyes burned. *Feeling sorry for our little selves, are we, Vivi?*

'Yes, we are,' she snapped then swore. Talking to that moron Rim in her head was bad enough but now she talked to him out loud as well! Get a grip, Viv, she castigated herself. Things could be a hell of a lot worse. The fold held things she loved like mountains, mist, and streams. It even had owls or what sounded like owls.

The cave was small but Viv checked it for rifts anyway. She found none but discovered someone had hollowed out a space behind the back wall. It was all but impossible to see unless you searched for it *or* for a rift. It would make an excellent hiding place and Viv wondered uneasily whether hiding places were necessary in the fold.

The cave's false back was not the only surprise. The light showed straight, wavy, and curling lines carved into the walls. Viv slid off the bracelet and held it up to the light. The patterns were not identical but they were close. Either it was a popular design or they had been made by the same person.

Viv heaved on the pack and stepped outside. It was still cool and misty with birdsong echoing eerily through the trees as she picked her way down to the stream. The whole area reminded Viv of when her mother had driven them high into the Ranges. They had eaten their sandwiches beside a swift flowing stream or, if it had been raining, sat in the car with the windows down.

Sometimes her mother had spoken of the Rockies where she had grown up, and of Ireland, where grandma Iris had been born and where great grandma Vacia and great, great grandma Rose had spent their girlhoods. But sometimes they had just sat and listened to the currawongs and bellbirds, and been at peace, safe from Jimmy Wright.

If Viv had not met Kald she could have served out her sentence and gone back to those mountains. Viv's mouth twisted. Who the hell was she kidding? Her education had ended at fourteen, her only qualifications were breaking and entering, *and* she had been in jail. Hardly the type of person a small town welcomed, let alone employed. She shrugged. It was irrelevant anyway given there was no way back.

The slope was slick and Viv took care not to slip especially on the boulders at the water's edge. The last thing she needed was a sprained ankle. The water rushed along with a music as clear as chimes and she stared up at the opposite bank. It was more a cliff than a bank and she was wondering whether it had more chance of caves *and* rifts when she heard voices.

She scrambled back up into the shelter of some trees but it was impossible to tell the direction the voices came from. One minute she was convinced the speakers were higher in the valley and the next, lower. If only the stinking mist would clear she could see what the hell was going on but then so could they.

Nothing happened and she had decided the speakers had gone when something moved on the opposite bank and the shadowy form of a man appeared. He came to the edge of the cliff and stared down at the water and Viv gasped. It was Thris!

He was naked to the waist, his immense black wings held aloft behind him, his face grave but more beautiful than she remembered. His perfect body was unmarked by the savagery she had seen inflicted on it and without conscious intent, she stepped into the open.

Thris's head swiveled and she caught the flash of violet eyes and heard a scythe of wings and then he was there and she flung herself into his arms. His sweetness was so potent her knees buckled but his arms locked her close and then she was airborne. He had flown her to the stream's other side but she only cared that he lived.

'I . . . I thought you were dead,' she choked. 'I saw what the cat creature did . . .'

'He was saved. Ash and I saved him.'

Viv started. It was Ky and she might have hugged him too but his expression stopped her. She glanced at Thris uncertainly. There was no hostility in *his* face but no joy either. He smiled, as if to compensate for Ky, but the smile was wooden. 'Ky and Ash took me to the Principae,' he said. 'They healed me as they healed you, then we returned to search for you.'

He smiled again but his eyes were blank and Viv's uneasiness grew. 'And now you've found me,' she said. Ky's antagonism was pretty bloody clear but Thris was harder to read. He was obviously relieved to find her given Kald's likely reaction to a hiccup in his grand plan for

94

transcendence but she wondered if Kald had sent Thris back too early.

He *looked* healed but not all damage was physical and Viv remembered a druggie she had fallen foul of. The woman had seemed normal, right up to the moment Viv had inadvertently challenged her and only then, when her hands had fastened around Viv's neck, had Viv noticed her pupils were as big as dinner plates.

It was also possible Thris had returned because Kald had threatened him, or because he felt guilty at mucking up the Guideship, but the last bloody thing she needed was a grudging Guide. 'Okay, let me get this straight,' she said. 'Kald sent you back even though he knows you tried to rape me?'

'Thris was undone by Moth Fold's corrosion,' broke in Ky. 'Not even an Archae could have withstood it!'

Viv kept her attention on Thris. 'Kald didn't think that you attacking his daughter was a problem?'

'I do not remember everything that occurred,' said Thris. 'But if I failed to beg your forgiveness at the time, I beg it now.'

'Well, I guess we can all move on then,' she said sarcastically. Kald certainly had. Apparently attempted rape was nothing in *his* scheme of things. Hardly bloody surprising given how he had treated her mother!

'We need to find a rift to continue our transits,' said Thris.

'No kidding?' said Viv. 'I was looking for a picnic spot.'

'A picnic spot?'

'Never mind,' she said, aware of Ky's glare. 'Let's get going.'

'Are you hungry? I have—'

'Just go,' snapped Viv. The slope meant they must walk

95

in single file and Thris led with Ky bringing up the rear. As well as *conveniently* forgetting his attempted rape, Thris had obviously forgotten she hated people behind her. It was probably an attempt to protect her, she grudgingly acknowledged, but she had survived a lot of shit on her own and did not need protection, especially from Ky.

Thris had bedded his wings but not even contemplating the superb musculature of his back soothed her temper. Rim had been broad shouldered and narrow-hipped too, and making love to him had been thrilling *at first*. It had just been sex, she corrected. Making love was something else entirely, although it had taken her a long time to learn the difference.

Chapter 18

Viv glanced over her shoulder as they walked and was relieved to see that Ky now watched the surrounding lands instead of sending her poisonous glances. He was shirtless like Thris and Viv was tempted to remove her jacket and let them guess why she wore her shirt halter style. They obviously intended to fly from threats, not pretend to be human, but they knew nothing about aggressive birdmen or drug-laden darts and she stopped and briefly outlined her experiences.

'It is safer to fly from danger than run,' said Ky, barely waiting for her to finish. 'I will carry you.'

'I have my own wings, as you know,' she said tartly.

'Ky told me of them,' said Thris. His voice was as emotionless as his face and Viv struggled to hide her disappointment. What the hell had she expected? That Thris would be ecstatic to have a mate worthy of him? A deluxe rather than base-model daimon? A daimon was still polluted by the crude stuff of human caste no matter how many wings it had and yet her wings were so beautiful and she had to resist the urge to flutter them under Thris's nose. It would annoy Ky if nothing else.

Ky did not want her coming between him and his best bud and the feeling was mutual but with Ky playing the protective pal, she could not get close enough to Thris to work out what was wrong with him. 'Are you still Shadow?' she asked Ky. He nodded. 'Then why aren't you travelling alone?'

'He aids me because I am not fully recovered,' said Thris. Ky threw him a grateful look and Viv gritted her teeth.

The gangs had resented women interfering with their *bonds of brotherhood* and it seemed angels were no different. 'If you're not fully recovered, Thris, why did your mentor, *who's supposed to guide and care for you*, send you back to the Rynth?'

'His concern for you was greater. It was imperative you were brought back under my protection.'

The idea that Kald gave a toss about her was so ridiculous Viv actually laughed. 'Kald only cares about his precious transcendence,' she said. '*You* should know that.' Neither Thris nor Ky made any response which was unsurprising. They were bound to obey higher angels but there was no way she was going to knuckle under and that meant quitting her girly dream of angel romance. 'Do you *actually* know where my mother is?' she demanded of Thris. It was a cruel question and one she already knew the answer to.

'No, but I am able to trace her through the Rynth.'

'But only if you can find a rift she used,' said Viv.

'That is correct.'

'But you can't find one, can you? In fact, this whole journey has been an effing disaster. First we get chased out of Hearth Fold into Moth Fold and I, at least, remember the shit that happened to me there, and then I end up with the cat creature. That was a hoot, I can tell you. Then the bloody thing tears you apart . . .' Viv's throat tightened but she struggled on. 'Then I go . . . to some place . . . full of sand that nearly suffocates me . . . then here, wherever *here* is . . .' She dashed the tears from her eyes and dragged in a breath. 'I'm not going *anywhere* with you, Thris. I've got as much chance of finding my mother on my own, as I have in your company, maybe more and you can tell that to my stinking father!'

Thris's face remained expressionless during her tirade but Ky's anger was palpable and she rounded on him. 'And *you'll* be happy to be rid of me so you can get back to your *boys' games* without me mucking them up!'

'You must stay with me, shekinah,' said Thris.

'*Shekinah*?' she choked out. 'You've even forgotten my name. It's Viv, Thris! Violet, Iris, Vacia! V-I-V! If you remember *nothing* else about me in all the eons to come, remember that!'

She stormed off through the trees, half-expecting Thris to force her back but she remained alone. Man-handling a *shekinah* was obviously against some angelic rule, she concluded savagely. If only screwing human caste women were too, she would not be in this shit-hole.

The mist showed no signs of lifting and she began to wonder if it were a permanent fixture or whether she had chosen a bad day. She followed the stream down, too angry to take any pleasure in it, and only knew the sun had set when the mist dulled. There was a cave on the slope above and she climbed up to it.

There were more wavy-line carvings inside but plenty of empty wall for Viv to scratch her own message. *Thris is a shit*, had a certain ring to it, except he was *not* a shit, he was *different* and there had been no time to work out how or why. If only—she cut the treacherous thought off. *Be careful what you wish for* . . . What a moronic saying that was. *Be careful what you wish for* or what? You got it and did not want it or you did not get it and wasted your life chasing it? Well, she had *not* got Thris . . . *except* for his feathers.

Bloody hell! She had forgotten all about them! She had an urge to fling them from the cavern's entrance and see where the wind took them but Thris had trained her too well. She would have to bury them but probably in the next fold as she did not have a shovel handy.

She settled against the cave's back wall, her gaze on the entranceway. Despite the words she had flung at Thris, finding her mother was going to take a massive stroke of luck and she had never been lucky.

Dusk gave way to darkness and as the birdsong faded, she closed her eyes, hoping for the oblivion of sleep. Then the air pulsed with sweetness and he was there, silhouetted in the entranceway, wings still beating. Viv did not move and he came to her and knelt, dusting her with his exquisite scent as he brought his lips to hers. Viv's mouth filled with a nectar that slid to the deepest parts of her being and she pulled him close. His touch woke her every sense and the more she drank from him, the more she thirsted.

She shrugged out of her clothes, beyond questioning what she did. His phallus was hard against her and then he brought his wings forward over them both. In the enclosed space, his sweetness was so potent it robbed her of reason and she was unaware even that he had entered her. All she knew was that in some place brilliant with stars, his essence had mixed with hers, and made them one.

Chapter 19

Viv woke to another chill, misty morning. She was alone, her jacket wrapped over her snuggly, but her clothes as scattered as she had left them. She dressed slowly, feeling hungover, not that she had ever been hungover. Living with Jimmy Wright had made her swear off alcohol for life.

She slung her pack over her shoulder and stared down at the stream. A black swan flapped in the water, which made no sense at all, and she blinked. It was Thris, thigh-deep in the stream as he rubbed at his body and beat his wings to dispel their wetness.

She started down the slope and flinched as Ky swooped to earth beside her. 'He scours away your foul taint, shekinah,' he said.

'Go to hell,' she retorted.

'You will destroy him!' hissed Ky and leapt skywards again.

Viv was more shaken by Ky's words than she cared to admit. 'Jealousy's a curse,' she muttered but the claim rang as hollow as everything else about Thris's return. He did not even offer her a smile when she reached him and Viv grimaced. She was used to cool receptions *the morning after* but most arseholes made *some* effort to hide their disinterest while Thris made none at all.

Why had he come after her anyway? Was it some sort of power game? *Offer the shekinah sex and she comes a-running*? This was not the angel who had nursed her after the glimmer attack; who had taught her to still her mind; who had flown her wet and shivering back to Haven after her dip in Glass Lake, his face full of tender concern.

He had made it abundantly clear sex was off the agenda for any angel who wanted to ascend.

And then there was Ky. He might be obnoxious but his love for Thris was real. *You will destroy him*, he had spat at her. None of it made sense. Thris had confessed to being tempted by her before and had fought the temptation until that terrible moment in Moth Fold and yet now he had seduced her, not that she had needed much seducing!

Thris was still bent at his ablutions and her blood roared as his wet skin gleamed. She had never wanted anyone like this before, not even Rim in their early days. No wonder her mother had risked everything for Kald.

Thris waded to shore and dressed but he only looked at her when he was about to heave his pack on and then only to ask if she were hungry. 'We will go then,' he said, when she shook her head, and started up the slope. He had always kept her in vision range and, after last night, she would have expected a brief touch at least, but there was nothing.

Despite Ky's claim, it might be Thris who destroyed *her*, Viv concluded, and let the gap widen to lessen the intensity of his scent. There was no reason to travel with him anyway, she told herself. She would go on alone as she had intended. Nothing had changed.

Rim's mocking laughter echoed in her head. *Oh, really Vivi? Ya had sex with a divine being and now ya can just trot off without a care in the world?* Viv scowled. If a Dane's chances of ascension *were* ruined by sex, Thris had just doomed himself, *unless* he had doomed himself in Moth Fold and having sex with her no longer mattered. He might even have had sex as payback for Kald's bullying, although given Thris had praised Kald's *protection* of her, it was unlikely.

Viv smiled grimly. There was one way to find out Thris's motives *and* prove once and for all whether angels lied and she quickened her steps and drew level. 'Why did you have sex with me?' she asked baldly.

'I thought it was what you wanted.'

'I wanted it way before Moth Fold. Why now?'

'I need to keep you safe.'

Viv blinked. 'You had sex with me to keep me with you?'

'Yes.'

Well, she had wanted honesty and she had got it. 'I kinda hoped you'd been blinded by my daimon beauty,' she said thickly.

'You *are* beautiful, shekinah, as exquisite as the Iahhel.'

His expression had gentled but Viv barely noticed. 'Oh, that's a relief,' she sneered. 'I thought you'd had to screw me with your eyes shut! But you've screwed your chances of ascension too, haven't you? I'd have thought Kald would have warned you about that.' And then her mouth went dry. 'He *told* you to screw me, didn't he?' Thris said nothing. 'Answer me!' she demanded furiously.

'In granting me the Guideship, Archae Kald entrusted me with your safety. I failed his trust once but in his grace, he gifted me a second chance to keep you safe.'

'By screwing me!'

'By using whatever means were necessary.'

Viv took several staggering steps away. Kald's betrayal of her was absolute but the violation went deeper than that. She had trusted Thris and Kald had used that trust against her *and* against Thris. She took several deep breaths. Well, her arsehole of a father was in for a surprise. She had survived a lot of bastards in her time and she would survive him *and* so would Thris.

She turned back. 'Kald doesn't give a shit about me or you. All he cares about is himself.'

'Archae Kald is not to blame for my failure,' said Thris. 'There is a flaw in me that was hidden for a time but would have revealed itself eventually. The Principae recognised it and appointed a Shadow. Ky will complete the Guideship and be rewarded with ascension.'

'And you?' she demanded. 'What about you, Thris?'

'All that matters is that Ky completes the Guideship.'

'Not to Kald,' said Viv bitterly. '*You* have to complete the Guideship or else his Brownie points for transcendence go down the toilet.'

Thris's face showed nothing but Viv sensed his turmoil. He was bound to Kald but loved Ky and he could not reconcile the two. But what was more shocking was Thris's lack of self-interest, in fact, it was worse than that, it was his self-loathing. She recognised it because she carried the same corrosion within her, but while hers was self-inflicted, Kald had inflicted it on Thris.

She reached for him but as he dutifully turned his head to meet her kiss she managed to tear herself away. Even so, a voice wheedled that having sex with him would be okay because it would be *her* choice, not Kald's, and she would be in control. *Oh sure, Vivi, in control like a druggie is*!

And the more times Thris *sinned*, the harder it would be for him to ascend and yet her need of him was scarcely bearable. She had never understood the nature of addiction *until now* and it would make journeying together a bloody nightmare. Yet she refused to let Kald use Thris then toss him aside like garbage.

'Shekinah . . .'

'It's Viv,' she said through clenched teeth.

'Viv.'

He said it as if he had never heard the name before and Viv wondered again just how damaged he was. He said the Principae had healed him *as they had healed her* but Thris had nursed her for what seemed weeks afterwards. Perhaps it was *her* turn to nurse *him*. Florence Nightingale to the rescue, she thought acidly.

'Viv, if my love-making has offended you—'

'It was the best sex I've ever had,' she said bluntly, 'but I'm not playing Kald's little game. I'll stay with you as long as—' And then there was a scream.

Chapter 20

It's Ky,' hissed Viv, gazing wildly at the empty slope. She wrenched off her jacket and Thris's eyes widened as she unbedded her wings.

'Stay here, shekinah, where it is safe,' he said urgently.

'No way! I'm—'

Ky screamed again and Thris's expression became agonised. 'I *must* keep you safe!'

'Then we go together! Now!' She launched skywards and sped in the direction of the screams then wings scythed as Thris loomed from the mist. It was thrilling to fly beside him, as if she were his equal after all.

'Stay close,' he ordered, and Viv nodded to placate him.

Something plunged from above and she yelled warning and swerved. The creature's momentum carried it past and she glimpsed an elongated bat-like face before it disappeared into the murk. Other shadowy shapes wheeled nearby. 'We need weapons,' she yelled and tore branches from a nearby tree. 'Stab or beat,' she instructed. 'Aim for the soft spots: eyes, ears, noses, genitals.'

'I must take you to safety,' cried Thris frantically.

'Watch out!' she shouted, and batted another creature away.

'Shekinah!' It was Ky, his call almost a howl.

She hovered, branch raised like a club. 'Where are you?' she yelled.

'I have him,' said Thris suddenly. 'This way, shekinah. Stay close!' At least Thris still had the skills to sense Ky's resonance and she sped after him. Ky was huddled in a tree, besieged by the creatures, and Thris beat them back so Viv could reach him. 'Keep to the trees as we fly out,' she instructed but Ky remained frozen, his wings bedded. 'We need to go,' she shrieked, ducking a creature's swoop. 'We'll have to carry him!' she yelled to Thris.

Thris grabbed one arm and she grabbed the other but they had not gone far before the creatures closed in. 'You take him,' she panted and thrusting Ky into Thris's arms, tore off more weapons from a passing tree and dropped back. She stabbed and swatted at the creatures then stifled a cry as yellow teeth raked her leg. But the creatures were not stupid and after a while stayed out of range and then, the mist was suddenly empty of them.

'We go to the cave,' panted Thris. 'It will be safer there.'

'I'm going to the stream first,' said Viv.

'You need to—'

'I won't be long,' she said and swerved away down slope. Pain shot up her leg as she landed and she stumbled into the water and scooped it over the wound. The wound was not deep but the creature's teeth had been filthy. The air moved and she whirled but it was Thris, his horrified gaze on her leg. 'It's nothing,' she said quickly. 'How's Ky?'

'Fearful but I needed to ensure your safety. Your leg, shekinah . . .'

'It's Viv, remember? And if Ky's distressed, it's best you stay with him.'

She went to move past him out of the water but he blocked her way, his attention on her wings and then, seemingly unaware of what he did, he reached out and touched them. Viv's brain berated her to put some distance between them but her legs refused to move.

'They are so beautiful,' he whispered. '*You* are so beautiful.'

Viv's breath caught not because of his words but because his face was as she remembered it, all woodenness gone. His wings curved forward and as hers rose in response, his black plumage covered her bronze and fluttered against it.

Frissons of heat surged through her body and she gasped as a burst of perfume was released so exquisite she climaxed in a single explosive jolt. Thris's wings quivered as they folded her close and she hung panting against him, aware that his chest heaved too, before she was lost in a brilliant sea of stars.

Dejon felt no surprise when the knock at his door revealed Kald. He knew it was just a matter of time before what happened in the folds came to the Archae's attention. He also knew that whatever Kald's intentions, he would ensure the Principae found them exemplary. What he did not know was how Kald planned to accomplish the feat.

Dejon smiled genially as he offered Kald refreshment and when Kald declined, filled his own goblet. The ambrosia was pleasant but not as pleasant as knowing the risks of what was to come lay entirely with Kald and *his* protégé, *and* that Kald's protégé was ill-equipped to manage them.

Kald spent no time on the courtesies expected of a meeting between Archae, not even deigning to sit. 'No doubt you are aware of the purpose of my visit, Archae,' he said as he held court from the centre of the room.

'On the contrary, I am baffled, Archae. Does it relate to the issue I raised with you some time ago that concerned the shekinah? The one you dismissed? Or perhaps to the issue Prime-archae Mirek raised? I believe he too was concerned about the shekinah, although I understand that again, it was not a concern you shared.'

'You are mistaken, Archae, if you believe my daughter's welfare is not of paramount importance to me. It is the reason I sent her Guide back into the Rynth at the earliest opportunity, despite his strength being less then fully restored. *He* understands, as *I* do, that my daughter's safety takes precedence over all else.'

'Given your protégé failed to protect the shekinah when his strength was unimpaired, it is difficult to see how your decision to send him back when his strength *is* compromised *will* ensure the shekinah's safety,' said Dejon, taking a leisurely sip from his goblet.

'Thrisdane has *many* strengths, as the Principae acknowledged in *choosing* to heal him. Brute strength is rarely effective in accomplishing difficult tasks, Archae, as you may or may not know.'

Dejon shrugged. 'Perhaps, although I would question whether the Principae *do* believe Thrisdane has the required qualities, however defined, given they appointed a Shadow.'

'*I* do not presume to know the intent of the Principae,' said Kald, 'although their assignation of a Shadow suggests they too are concerned with my daughter's safety, which brings me to the reason for my visit. As I believe you have known *for some time*, my daughter is winged which indicates greater angelic essence than is usual for daimon.

'I have reflected on my sojourns in Moonsun as a lesser Archae and on the fact that, unlike Ezam, Moonsun Fold has many sectors,' continued Kald. 'This confusion of places, coupled with the time disparities between the folds, raises the possibility of me having fathered my daughter more than once.'

Dejon drained his goblet and rose. 'Or not at all,' he replied pleasantly. 'Since *my* protégé reported the presence of wings I have, of course, considered their likely cause *and* taken advice from Prime-archae Serith who, despite the effects of the Black Obsidian Stele, retains the most thorough knowledge of angelic lore.'

Dejon sauntered to the window and glanced out before turning back. 'Prime-archae Serith agrees that a winged daimon must be birthed by a daimon, although that is the limit of his present wisdom. Having had *considerable* time to review the nature of my *immature* dalliances, and the relative importance of human and angel caste elements, the only explanation is that *I* seeded the shekinah *and* her mother too.'

Kald's eyebrows rose. 'Even a Dane might deduce that a daimon with wings has high levels of angel essence bequeathed from *both* parents,' said Kald. 'I have an excellent memory which is fortunate, for I have no need of *considerable* time to know *your* recollections are flawed, that is, *if* you really believe your dalliance with Rose resulted in *my* daughter.'

Dejon gave an exaggerated frown. 'Rose?'

'My daughter's mother,' gritted Kald.

'*My* daughter's mother was called Lettie,' said Dejon, with a gentle smile. 'The shekinah herself confirmed the name, when I questioned her directly, in the presence of *your* protégé.'

It was Kald's turn to shrug. 'Moonsun human caste call themselves all manner of names,' he said dismissively. 'They change them on partnering or on a whim. As I reminded you last time you sought to claim my daughter, scent and resonant print are surer markers of parentage, and mine are strong in the shekinah.'

110

'As are mine which is possibly another reason the Principae appointed *my* protégé Shadow. For it follows, does it not, Archae, that my daughter should remain under my care, through *my* protégé, in her journey to her mother?'

'As I have said, *I* do not presume to know the Principaes' intent even if *you* do, Archae, but I am well versed in my obligations to preserve the harmony of the Rynth. Now that the presence of wings in my daughter has been *belatedly* brought to my attention, I must pass her into the Principae's care. As I am sure you are aware, Archae, a daimon more Iahhel than human caste cannot be directed by any member of the Host, not even by the member who fathered her.'

'And how exactly do you intend to discharge your obligations?'

'Prime-archae Serith, the angel with the *most thorough knowledge of angel lore*, claims the blue angel, Ashdane, communicates with my protégé in the folds. Through Ashdane, I will order Thrisdane to immediately return my daughter to Ezam.' Kald paused. 'Of course, those who *claim* the blue angel has this facility might have erred, as they have erred in other matters,' he added with a frosty smile.

'And if Ashdane is unable to communicate?'

'Surely you do not suggest those who *claim* this special talent for him, and those who *believe* such claims, have done so without proper investigation? However, if their judgements *are* flawed, I will seek guidance directly from the Principae.'

'Perhaps it would be wise to seek guidance from the Principae sooner,' said Dejon. 'Given the doubt over the shekinah's parentage, they might deem you lack the authority to proceed as you intend.'

Kald drew himself up to his full height. 'There is *no* doubt over my daughter's parentage although there is considerable doubt over your judgement! If you would like the Principae to assess *that*, then you are as free as any of the Host to seek their advice. As your protégé travels with mine and is affected by what is to come, I have merely extended the courtesy of informing you of my intentions. Now that I have done so, I will inconvenience you no longer.'

Chapter 21

The door slammed and Dejon poured himself more ambrosia as Kald's footsteps echoed away. Kald had done his usual excellent job of turning his vices into virtues but the truth was a somewhat different matter.

Kald had made no attempt to familiarise himself with the shekinah and so remained ignorant of her true, headstrong nature which was likely to impact his plans. To make matters worse, he had chosen a Guide with insufficient strength to withstand the demands of the Guideship and, when the Guide had inevitably failed and returned shockingly injured, Kald had forced him back into the folds. And now, despite having pledged to reunite the shekinah with her mother, Kald intended to hand over to the Principae.

Dejon's tongue flicked along his lips. The success of Kald's strategy depended on his ability to return the shekinah to Ezam, which in turn depended on Ashdane relaying Kald's orders to the Guide, and the Guide having the strength to carry them out. It also relied on Kald having the authority, *as the shekinah's father*, to act.

Dejon drained his goblet and returned to the window. Ezam's sky was a delicate peach unlike the blue, grey and black skies of Moonsun Fold. The coming and going of that fold's light had fascinated Dejon, as had its glittering stars that hinted at the Great Beyond.

Kald claimed it was the time discrepancies between folds that had caused him to father the shekinah more than once and it was possible, for it was exactly what Dejon *had* done by enjoying sexual congress with the shekinah's mother *and* members of her ancestral line. Dejon drained his goblet and turned back to the jug but it was empty and he was glad. Ambrosia clouded the mind when imbibed to excess and that was the last thing he needed now.

It would be a mistake to dismiss Kald's claims as arrogant glory-seeking, although Dejon little doubted they sprang from such base emotions. The fact was that for his own aggrandisement, Kald had sought his scent and resonant print in the shekinah and found them and, Dejon admitted uncomfortably, he had sought his own scent and resonant print in the shekinah, and found them too.

But then another shocking possibility presented itself, that they might *both* have fathered the shekinah multiple times and that meant she might have many times more angel essence than either of them thought. 'Iahhel,' he groaned, and shut his eyes.

Prime-archae Mirek had just finished his instructions to Kald's messenger on how to reach the Blue Helixai when Dejon's messenger appeared and he repeated his instructions and watched the second Dane set off back through the shelves.

'I fear neither of them will find Ashdane,' said Mirek as he rejoined Serith at the table. 'The Blue Helixai has many caverns and I am unclear which Ashdane favours. The Archaes would be better advised to wait for Ashdane to return here and for *me* to pass on their orders but apparently both Archaes' needs are urgent.'

Serith slowly re-rolled the scroll he had examined and placed it back on the shelf. 'Ezam has no mechanisms to deal with urgency,' he said. 'It is a place of contemplation, not of action.'

'Not an observation I will pass onto the Archaes,' said Mirek tersely. 'While I cannot presume to know their intentions, I suspect both wish to use Ashdane to communicate with their respective protégés.'

'In the end, Senquar-archae chose not to serve those more highly placed,' said Serith, busy perusing the shelves. 'His sudden absence caused much consternation.'

Mirek straightened. 'You have read more of him?'

'Fragments here and there. No one scroll gives a complete history, as if those who wrote of him did so furtively. Obviously Senquar-archae's absence avoided the imposts of those such as Archae *and* spared his friends the backwash of his transformation.'

'His friends' ascension was adversely affected?' asked Mirek sharply.

'That I have not read,' said Serith as he brought an armful of scrolls back to the table. He unrolled the first and examined it intently but Mirek felt too unsettled to resume his own scholarship. He heard the rustle of others as they moved between the shelves but his attention remained on Serith. 'Ashdane grows stronger, but I wonder if, in the end, he will be strong enough,' murmured Serith as he stared down at the scroll.

'Strong enough for what?' demanded Mirek. Since Serith's return to his studies, Mirek sensed the Black Obsidian Stele had gifted him powerful insights, but extricating them from his friend was not easy.

'The Principae do not bequeath white plumage lightly,' said Serith with unusual clarity. 'It must be earned over the eons and yet Ashdane has white in his wings. He has been tested and his testing will continue, but greatly compressed and so more violent. His transcendence will be swift or not at all.'

Mirek opened his mouth to speak but shut it again as he understood the truth of Serith's words. Ashdane had not fully revealed what he experienced in the Blue Helixai but had spoken of the Red and Mirek knew of his flight through the rifts to retrieve Thrisdane. Mirek also knew what it had cost Ashdane to reunite the Guide with his Shadow.

Mirek stared down at the scroll on the table and wondered whether Ashdane had already removed himself from the Host's company and if he had, whether Mirek would be sad or relieved. Loyalty versus self-interest, he mused wryly. Always an interesting conundrum.

Ash knew when the Dane had entered the Blue Helixai and when the Helixai had rearranged itself to trap them in different tunnels. He knew of their terror too and sent them soothing thoughts, then coaxed the stone to release them and visioned them flap away. But he did not leave his resting place in the Helixai's heart, nor rouse sufficiently to wonder at his power.

He was aware of Ezam's sky cycling through peach and umber, of the bloom and drop of glis blossoms, of Dane that streaked through the Hollow Hills in trials, but he was removed from it and it was only a vague sense of thirst that made him to quit the slab and make his way to the outer cavern.

His gaze was drawn to the White Helixai but he sensed much time had passed and that Prime-archae Mirek might wonder why his friend had ceased to visit. He winged away in the direction of the Bokos and was almost there when he sensed an ambrosia font, came to ground and drank.

Awareness grew of its wetness in his mouth, of its

fragrant sweetness, then of the chiming of the surrounding glis, and of bright flashes of sumi, and he continued on foot, keen to reacquaint himself with the crunch of glis leaves and the tangle of succulent vines.

He reached the Bokos and made his way deeper into the gloom, carrying his wings aloft and oblivious to the gasps of startled Du- and Prime-archaes as his senses ranged ahead in search of Prime-archae Mirek. The Prime-archae's greeting was warm but Ash's time with him brief for the Prime-archae had orders from Archaes Kald and Dejon to send Ashdane to them immediately on his return.

'At least you have a choice as to which Archae you visit first,' said Mirek with a smile.

Ash's guess that the summons involved Thris and Ky was correct but while both Archaes required the shekinah be returned to Ezam, Archae Kald stipulated that Thris be responsible for the task and Archae Dejon that Ky be responsible for Thris's completion of the task. It was a subtle but important difference and reflected the mentors' wishes to garner merit for their own protégés and themselves.

Ash was glad of their orders for it meant Thris would return to Ezam to complete his healing and Ky would be spared the dangers of the rifts. And best of all, the three of them would be together again.

Swift wingbeats returned him to the Blue Helixai and he stretched out on the slab. The first time Ash *dreamed,* Thris had been in Beast Fold and reaching him had taken many cycles but now he slipped into the same state quickly. A white haze replaced the blue stone and as the dream sharpened, the haze drifted in a landscape treed like the Dendrinai but steep like the Hollow Hills.

A narrow lake of rushing water distracted him and when he dragged his attention from the extraordinary sight, he sensed his friends' *and* the shekinah's resonance but his relief was short-lived; Ky's resonance was contorted by terror.

Chapter 22

Viv watched the bright rush of water as she walked but her entire attention was on Thris. It was as if they were connected by a silver cord woven from sweet resonance and starry brilliance and humming with an understanding that was both mental and physical. He walked behind her with Ky but Viv knew his thoughts, not as a mind-reader might, but as a pattern of intent threaded through with shining threads of emotions. She knew he wanted to lead, that his Guideship demanded it, and that he struggled to reconcile it with Ky's need for comfort.

Her human part yearned for the sight of him but when she glanced back all she saw was Ky's set face and his arms clamped about himself in fear. He must be *really* scared to walk so close to the *foul* shekinah but she felt sorry for him. She knew what it was to have fear twist your stomach like a knife. She wanted Ky back in Ezam for his sake but she mainly wanted Thris to herself.

Sex suckered ya principles, Vivi? Rim's sarcasm triggered yet another churn through all that had happened. Thris had seduced her *under orders* the first time but Viv wondered if their second encounter had even sex. *With an orgasm like that, Vivi? Who ya kiddin'?* The first time had hurt Thris as much as her but the second time had healed something in them both, yet logic told her both incidents had damaged Thris's chances of ascension.

Sex was sex regardless of people's motivations and she did not want to hurt him *or* help her arsehole of a father clamber up the last few rungs to heaven. She must keep her resolve to stay away from Thris but as the silvery cord hummed sweetly between them, she had no idea how.

They stopped for a rest at what Viv guessed was midday, but the mist made it hard to tell. Ky collapsed onto a stone and stared blankly at the water and Viv continued a little way along the bank. She needed to put space between her and Thris but he followed, his magnificent face so full of tenderness it all but undid her.

'Ky's no better,' she said, forcing her gaze past him to where the other angel sat. 'Given his fear of folds, I'm surprised he was made Shadow.'

'I do not presume to know the Principae's purpose but Ezam holds no threats and so fear remains unfamiliar. Some angels are overwhelmed when they first encounter it.'

'You haven't been overwhelmed,' said Viv.

Thris's eyes darkened with pain. 'Not by fear,' he said.

Viv ran the backs of her fingers down his cheek, relieved to see amethyst seep back and he caught her hand and kissed her palm. 'You should take Ky back to Ezam,' she said thickly. 'He's a danger to himself *and* to us.'

'My Guideship requires me to take you to your mother and Ky's duty as Shadow requires him to accompany us. He can return to Ezam if he chooses, for the Principae do not force, but I cannot make the decision for him. My only authority over him is as a friend.'

'Then friendship dictates you take him back,' persisted Viv.

Thris did not respond and Viv sensed the conflict of his divided loyalties again *and* his surge of desire. Their wings were bedded but the air frissoned and Thris drew her into his arms. 'I don't want to hurt you,' she whispered.

'How could you hurt me?'

'By having sex with you, by damaging your chances of ascension.'

'I sense your essence heals rather than harms me,' he said softly. 'I feel—'

'Thris!' shrieked Ky. His hands were clamped to his temples and they hastened back. 'Thris,' he groaned, rocking backwards and forwards.

'What is it? Are you in pain?' asked Thris urgently.

'It is Ash,' whispered Ky, white-faced. 'He is speaking inside my head!'

'Ash spoke to me like that in Beast Fold. What does he say?'

Ky's eyes widened. 'He says Archae Dejon commands me to return and to ensure you return as well. He says Archae Kald's orders are the same. We are to take the shekinah back to Ezam.' Ky smiled tremulously. 'We are going home, Thris.'

'I'm not going back,' said Viv.

'Does Ash say *why* we are to return?' asked Thris.

'No. He has stopped speaking now.' Ky scrambled up and gripped Thris's arm. 'It does not matter *why*, Thris. The Archaes' orders are clear.'

'No one's heard these orders except you,' said Viv.

'Angels do not lie,' said Thris sharply.

'Even ones crapping themselves with fear?' demanded Viv. 'Even ones—' She stopped as something moved upslope. Shapes emerged from the mist, small and roughly clad, human but with inhumanly long arms. The dwarves of fairytale, thought Viv nonsensically, with the arms of monkeys.

They advanced slowly and stopped, and in the hiatus that followed, Viv noticed they had small, hooded eyes, almost flat noses, and lipless mouths, then Ky gave a strangled cry and bolted. There was an answering bellow from the monkey-dwarves and rocks pelted down. Viv felt the shock as they struck her and one glanced off Thris's forehead, drawing blood.

'Run!' she shrieked.

They sped after Ky along the bank, leaping mossy stones and dodging holes and driftwood. Viv considered shrugging off her pack and jacket and taking to the air, but somewhere ahead Ky was on the ground, too panicked to think. The mist thickened until it was fog and although no more rocks were hurled, she noticed shadowy forms moving on their left flank. The monkey-dwarves seemed content to lope beside them, pinning them against the stream as if they herded them like *lambs to the slaughter*.

But before she could warn Thris, his head swiveled. 'Ky's fallen,' he cried, and sprinted off ahead.

The fog swallowed him and Viv's fear ratcheted up. 'Thris,' she shouted. 'Wait!' Beyond her pounding heart she heard the roar of falling water and slewed to a stop, arms wind-milling, pebbles spinning into space. The stream had plunged into a fog-filled abyss. 'Thris!' she screamed, but there was no answer.

Ash gazed across the hazy distance to the White Helixai's glimmering peak. Thris had delighted in its light-filled caverns but their visits seemed long ago and he moved restlessly as he sensed the immense age of the blue stone behind him, of Ezam's lands, and of himself. Was this how Archae felt as they neared transcendence? And the Principae, as they cast off their last vestiges of flesh?

Ash's thoughts were so odd he wondered if they stemmed from exhaustion but his mental forays to other folds troubled him less than the Archaes' orders and he feared what they might demand next. The Blue Helixai not only gifted him a heightened awareness of Ezam's beauty but of the murkier depths of the Archaes' lofty motives and while no Dane could presume to judge an Archae, he yearned to distance himself from them.

He knew he should inform the Archaes their orders had been delivered *and* visit Prime-archae Mirek but the White Helixai's peak held him and, as his focus on it narrowed, a great plume of frosty fire shot high into the air. Ash's breath caught and he launched from the Blue Helixai and flew in its direction.

Chapter 23

Viv screamed Thris's name again as she teetered on the edge of the cliff and heard a faint reply. She had no idea how far down he was *or* where, or whether he was injured. A rock whistled past her head and she dropped onto her backside and let go, was briefly airborne, then landed with a bone-jarring crunch, skewed sideways, and picked up speed.

Gnarled trees rushed past and she grabbed at one, missed and managed to grab the next. The branch all but tore free but she stopped and, hoping to hell it held, clawed her way up it, wedged herself between the tree and the cliff to shed her jacket, and took to the air.

She called to Thris as she flew and he answered but the fog bounced the sound around and she frantically swept the cliff face. Shapes loomed from the murk, morphed into terrifying monkey-dwarves, and back into thorn-laden bushes and in desperation, she hovered and sensed for him.

Something hummed on the edge of her awareness and strengthened as a shadowy cave emerged in the cliff face. A rift! Viv all but swooned in relief. The cave might be thick with thorny bushes but it was a way out and even better was Thris's resonance that rippled up from below it.

He was almost vertical, his back against the cliff, his feet wedged against a narrow ledge as he cradled an unconscious Ky. Thris had gashes on his forehead and cheek and his perch was so precarious he could not move enough to unbed his wings.

'There's a rift above,' she said hurriedly. 'Let me take Ky. We need to fly up.'

Viv's wings beat hard as she took Ky's weight and Thris shrugged off his pack and jacket. 'The rift might not take us where we need to go,' he warned as his magnificent wings unfurled. Viv's shimmered in response and she fought a surge of desire. Not now, she castigated herself. Concentrate on saving your sorry arse, not satisfying it!

Thris took Ky back and they flew up to the cave but the bushes were so thick she had to cradle Ky again while Thris bedded his wings to fight a way through. He needed a machete, she thought, as she peered nervously into the fog. And then grit rained down! 'They're coming!' she shrieked and half threw Ky into Thris's arms. He hauled Ky to safety as a monkey-dwarf leapt from the murk and fastened itself onto Viv's jacket. She tore herself free but then the cliff face was crawling with them.

She flew clear and as Thris fought to repel them, attacked them from behind, catching their arms or legs and hurling them into space, but they kept coming. 'Viv!' cried Thris, as a mass of monkey-dwarves swarmed between them.

'Go!' she screamed and glimpsed his anguished face before something slammed into her and she plunged away through the whiteness. A monkey-dwarf had clamped itself about her shoulders, its bristly hide harsh against her cheeks. She wrenched it off but it latched onto her wings instead.

Visions of Thris's wing being all but torn off rushed back and she bedded them in an instant dropped like a stone. A tree loomed from the fog and she smacked through its branches, hit the ground, and took off down slope on her back. The monkey-dwarf had gone but then she was airborne again as she plummeted through clammy whiteness into sunshine. A river glittered below her, then above her, then below her. *Unbed your wings*! a voice in her head shrieked then stopped as she slammed into water.

Thris staggered from the rift, lowered Ky to the ground, and wept. The rift still thrummed behind him, still provided a way back to Viv, but Ky lay motionless. 'Ky?' he whispered but Ky did not stir. The new fold was coming out of its dark cycle; jagged mountains silhouetted against a red sky, emerging from the gloom. It might be Redice Fold or another of the uncountable folds in the Rynth but Ky needed shelter.

Thris picked him up and set off towards the mountains, tears wetting his face as each step took him further from Viv, and he had not gone far before he sensed a second rift. Rest and safety lay at its other end but he longed for the sweetness that had healed his deepest wounds, made him whole, redeemed him.

'Viv,' he groaned and then he looked down and love for his injured friend surged anew. 'We are going home, Ky,' he whispered, and stepped into the rift.

Viv lay sprawled on the ground, too overwhelmed by hopelessness to move. Thris had gone, the sweet silver cord that had bound them, torn in two. She kept her eyes closed, unable to bear a future empty of his presence, but scent dragged her back, not to the present, but to the country town of her childhood.

It had almost been wiped out by a bush fire and Viv had passed smouldering paddocks and burned cars on her walk to school. The burnt smell was nothing like the smell of a campfire or a cheery hearth; it was acrid, like here.

Viv opened her eyes. She was saturated and covered in soot. She lifted her head and groaned. There was no part of her that did not hurt but considering her trip down the cliff, it was a miracle nothing was broken. She groaned again as she sat up. The sky was a dismal grey, either dawn or dusk, or maybe a version of Moth Fold's sepia. Whatever the case, it made things even bleaker.

She cranked herself upright and wiped the soot from her eyes. She was surrounded by burned buildings and the stench of putrefying meat. Animals took the brunt of bush fires and Viv remembered the burned kangaroos tangled in barbed-wire fences and the sheep with flesh hanging off their backs.

The cops had shot them and while Viv had no gun, she refused to leave any animal to suffer a slow, agonising death. She trawled the wreckage for a solid piece of timber and limped in the direction of the smell. It came from the lee of a charred wall and she cautiously peered around. Injured animals could cause a lot of damage in their fear and pain but there were no injured animals, just the charred and mutilated corpses of men, women, and children. Viv reeled backwards and her gaze took in her surroundings *untouched by fire*. She was not in a bushfire area, she realised in horror, she was in a war zone!

Chapter 24

She stumbled to the shelter of the nearest tree and collapsed against it. Her last memory was of plunging towards a river and her wet clothes told her she had landed in it, but she was not in it now, nor could she see any water. The only explanation was she had somehow bull's-eyed a water rift. And her pack was gone! Shit! Shit! Shit!

It was probably at the bottom of the river, wherever that was, along with everything else she needed *and* Thris's feathers. She clutched at her throat, and closed her eyes in relief; the twist of material was still there.

She leaned her head back against the tree. Thris would take Ky back to Ezam and then return to search for her but a few minutes in Ezam could be a lifetime here and that was assuming he had made it back to Ezam in the first place. He might have ended up somewhere worse or been overwhelmed by the monkey-dwarves and killed.

The silver cord was definitely gone *and* the pack, which left her with the sodden, soot-covered clothes she stood up in and the hope Thris would return. *Hey Vivi, maybe the next transit will deliver ya to a posh hotel and put a credit card in ya pocket*, Rim's voice mocked.

'Hey Rim,' she muttered, 'maybe the next transit will deliver me to a fold without your crappy voice.'

The burned-out settlement was surrounded by steep, wooded slopes and she started to climb, desperate to get away from the carnage and any murderous thugs who still might loiter. The climb was hard but she was rewarded by the crimson sunrise of a single sun that slowly turned the sky blue. There was birdsong too, like the previous fold, and the spicy smell of things that grew.

Viv perched on a rocky outcrop to catch her breath. It gave her a good view of the surrounding lands and a better understanding of why Thris disliked human caste folds. A black scar deeper in the trees marked a second charred settlement and a pall of smoke rose from beyond the next ridge.

She screwed her head around and scanned the rock face above. 'Bingo,' she whispered. The cave was a long way up and she soon discovered the climb needed the strength of someone who had not fought off monkey-dwarves and bounced down a cliff. It was close to dusk before she reached it although she smelled it first and wondered if it were full of grubs like Moth Fold. It was not; it was full of human excrement. Even the walls were smeared with it and to finish the job, someone had taken to them with a hammer.

Her first instinct was to get the hell out of there but there were carvings under the excrement similar to those in the birdman's fold, and her breath emptied. Either it was one almighty coincidence or she was still in the same fold.

Thris had said nothing about rifts operating *within* folds so maybe it *was* a coincidence *unless* the cave had a false back. Holding her nose, she picked her way through the filth and then the air hummed. 'Bingo again,' she muttered. 'Maybe this rift won't take me to a posh hotel, Rim, but I'll settle for one empty of shit and suffering.'

She was tempted to take the rift out immediately but it would be handy to know if rifts *did* open and close in the same folds. The cave back had been hollowed out, which seemed to answer the question, but as she peered sideways into the space another set of eyes peered back. God in Heaven! It was a child.

The child was obviously a survivor from the burned-out settlement but Viv had nothing to offer: no food, no water, and certainly no safety. She could take the child with her, she supposed, but there was no guarantee either of them would survive the next fold and the child might have family here somewhere. It would be best to leave them to find their own way to safety. *Yeah sure, Vivi, like those in the burned-out settlement had.* Viv chewed her lip as she glanced back towards the rift. Thris said rifts could stay open for eons or snap shut in an instant. *Stay or leave, Vivi, make an effing decision.*

Viv squatted so she was on the child's level. 'Are you going to come out?' she asked. 'I won't hurt you.' She had almost said *trust me* but why the hell should the child trust her? The child did not move and Viv settled her backside on the floor, careful to avoid the crap. If the rift closed, so be it; she could not leave a child cowering in a hole.

Time stretched and as the cave dimmed, Viv leaned her head back against the stone. God how she wanted to be away from here! The bastards who had burned the settlement might be on their way back to add more shit to the cave. Maybe she should simply drag the child out. Yeah, great idea, Viv. Nothing like force to build trust.

'I know what it's like to be frightened,' she said softly. 'To be so scared even breathing is agony. I know what it's like to want to screw yourself down so deep into a hole that you disappear. I'm scared now. I don't want to be here, but I'm a stranger in these parts. I don't know where to go that's safe. Maybe you could show me.'

There was a furtive rustling as the child moved for the first time and Viv held her breath. 'What are you named?' the child asked.

A girl's voice speaking English with a slight roll of the *r*'s. 'I am named Viv,' said Viv, using the same phrasing.

'En-Valen?'

'Just Viv,' said Viv, having no idea what *en-valen* meant. She paused. 'And what are you named?'

No response. Maybe having no answer to *en-valen* was a deal breaker. The cave was all but dark and there would soon be no way of exiting without stepping in crap. Then she would be covered in soot *and* shit. The little girl remained untrusting, which was a problem, but it was also most likely why she had survived.

When Jimmy Wright had shouted and smashed things, her mother had held Viv in the darkness and sung to her, Irish songs full of wild, sweet yearnings that came from great, great grandma Rose.

Viv could not remember the words but she remembered the tunes and she hummed them to comfort herself as much as the child and slowly the child crept out and then astonishingly, onto Viv's lap. Viv brought her arms around her and the child cried, deep heart-rending sobs that tore at Viv's heart. Viv held her close but did not speak. What was there to say? Everything will be okay? Things will go back to the way they were? The dead will rise? The little girl quieted until there was only the occasional sniff, but Viv continued to hold her, comforted by her warmth and softness.

'You smell like da,' the child murmured sleepily, as she nestled deeper into Viv's arms.

Da must smell like soot and sweat then, thought Viv, but she feared *da* lay amongst the corpses below. The little girl said no more and her breathing told Viv she had slipped into sleep.

The stars' brilliance increased outside until they striped the cave's entrance with shadows and Viv watched them as she searched for ways to rid herself of the child that did not stink of abandonment. She gave up and tried to think of more pleasant things but that did not work either and she was relieved when bird song finally heralded the dawn.

Light spilled in to reveal the little girl's fine featured face, her dark brows, and long dark braid, but she was too dirty for Viv to tell how fair-skinned she was. She wore a tunic top and trousers of fine weave with patterning around the neck and cuffs. They were dirty too but at least they looked warm.

The child's eyes opened but she did not look up, simply stared straight ahead. 'Time to go,' said Viv expecting the little girl to clamber from her lap but she clung on more tightly. Like a little a monkey, thought Viv, as she struggled to her feet and then recalling the monkey-dwarves, amended it to *possum*.

Sitting on stone all night had not helped Viv's battered muscles and she picked her way stiffly through the filth. The rift still hummed but she forced herself on past it. The little girl buried her face in Viv's shoulder as if she could not face the day and Viv felt scarcely better. Yesterday's smoke had gone but the ruined settlements were stark among the trees and Viv wondered whether *any* settlements had survived and if so, whether she could deliver the little girl there and get back before the rift closed.

'I've lost my shoe,' the little girl said, and stuck out her bare foot. Viv glanced down but she did not see the little girl's grubby foot; she saw the other child's shoe, the oil-sheened bitumen, and the broken windscreen glass. 'Are you going to leave me here?' the little girl asked in a small voice.

'No, I'm going to take you to those who love you,' said Viv as solemnly as if she swore an oath. 'But I don't know the way.'

'We need to go up,' the little girl said.

Viv stared up at the rocky cliff. 'So be it,' she muttered and set off.

Chapter 25

It was midday before Viv stopped, set the child down, and flopped down on a stone. She ached from her battle with the monkey-dwarves and carrying the little girl up the mountain was exhausting. It was still a fair way to the top too. The child sat beside her in silence, so untrusting Viv did not even know her name. She also feared the little girl would bolt now her terror had worn off. *Save ya a lot of trouble if she did*, Rim's voice intruded.

Probably, conceded Viv, but the child was still a lot safer with her. Viv's time on the streets had taught her some handy skills although conjuring meals was not one of them. 'I don't have any food,' she admitted, 'but we should drink before we go on.'

The little girl disappeared through scrubby bushes below and Viv hurried after her, cursing her sore muscles, and stopped in astonishment. There was a steep-sided gully, invisible from above, where water slid from the stone to disappear into mossy boulders. The whole area was thick with ferns.

The child cupped the waterfall in her hands, emptied it over the stones to her left, then right, washed her hands and face vigorously and only then did she drink. She looked at Viv expectantly and Viv followed suit. It was some sort of thanking ritual, she guessed, and she *was* thankful to wash away the filth from the crap-filled cave. She was not thirsty but drank so the child would not think her odd. 'It's pretty here,' said Viv.

'Eshavale's the most beautiful of all the Vales,' the little girl boasted.

'How many Vales are there?' asked Viv and mentally kicked herself. The child *would* think her odd if she did not even know that, but the child did not seem to notice, just recited the list of Vales in a sing-song voice.

'Eshavale, Ascavale, Genessavale, Beshavale, Terissavale, Sonoravale, Morvavale, Warinavale.' Then her dark eyes came to Viv's. 'En-Valen?'

It was the same question she had asked earlier but now Viv understood its meaning. 'I'm not from the Vales,' she said and wished for the umpteenth time she could lie.

The little girl's eyes widened. 'You're Astraali?'

For a moment Viv thought the child had said *Australian,* and her heart missed, but it was the child's lilt and Viv shook her head. 'I'm a stranger in these parts.'

The child looked about ten and Viv tried to remember how she had made sense of the world as a ten-year-old. It had been when her mother had disappeared and all Viv could recall was loneliness and fear. She lowered her backside onto a mossy stone so their faces were level. 'I was travelling with a friend,' she began, ignoring the wet seep through her pants. 'We were attacked and during the fight I fell. When I woke up I was in the burned-out settlement below. I was frightened and wanted to hide so I climbed into the hills. I saw the cave and thought it would be a good place to stay until I felt better. Then I found you.'

The gaps in her story were big enough to drive a fleet of trucks through and the little girl's doubt was plain. 'Where's your friend now?' she asked.

'I don't know,' said Viv.

'What's your friend named?'

'Thris.' Beautiful, beautiful Thris. Where the hell are you? The little girl tensed and Viv struggled to calm.

135

'You have funny names,' the little girl said. 'Short, like horses' names.'

'My friend's name is really Thrisdane and mine's Violet Iris Vacia, which is pretty long.' Viv forced a smile. 'Where I come from, we like to shorten names. What are you named?'

'Da said not to tell anyone.'

The little girl was fearful again and Viv nodded reassuringly. '*Da* is your father?' she asked. The child nodded. 'Well,' said Viv, 'your da probably has good reason for telling you that but I need to call you *something*. How about I call you Poss? It's short for possum which is a cute furry little animal.'

The child said nothing and Viv stood and eased her soggy pants away from her skin. 'You must be hungry,' she said with forced lightness. 'Is there something nearby we can eat? Nuts or berries?'

'There's blackbor,' said Poss and wrinkled her nose. 'I'll wait till we get home.'

'Home?' said Viv, in surprise. 'Is that close?'

'We have to cross Eralia Ridge and then Serier, but I'm a good climber. Da says so.'

'This is Eralia we're climbing now?' asked Viv hopefully. Poss nodded. 'And Serier's about the same height?' Another nod. Viv pushed her curls from her eyes and tried to calculate how long they would take to cross. Too long for a child without food, she concluded anxiously.

They clambered out of the gully and Viv picked up Poss up but was forced to set her down again when the slope steepened. The climb would be a hell of a lot quicker if Poss could walk *and* if they had food. Viv clutched at the feather around her neck. If only she had

136

not lost the pack! Well, she would just have to make Poss a shoe from what she *did* have.

She tore several strips from the bottom of her shirt and using a layer of grass as a sole, wound the material around Poss's foot. 'Maybe I should have called you Cinderella,' she said, as she fastened the ends in a ragged bow.

'*Sindarella*?'

'A girl in a story who lost her shoe,' said Viv briefly and wondered whether mentioning Cinderella was transference. If it were, it was a small thing compared with Viv being there.

'Da tells me stories. Will you tell me about Sindarella?'

'Later,' promised Viv. 'After we cross that ridge.'

As the day wore on, Viv wondered whether she would ever get to tell the tale of the girl who used magic to snare her Prince Charming. The climb seemed never-ending. She could use a little magic herself, she thought sourly, such as a fairy godmother to magic-wand her to the top. The slope was as steep as a cliff in places and Viv's thoughts turned to the monkey-dwarves. At least there was no fog to hide them but she and Poss were visible too.

If only she had not found a child! She could have been far from here by now, perhaps even back with Thris. Viv clutched the feather at her throat as she recalled his anguish as the monkey-dwarves swarmed between them. They *would* be together again, she asserted fiercely, even if it took years.

The setting sun painted the stone as red as the Outback and Viv wondered again whether she had transited home.

Despite what Thris had said, it might be possible to go back *if* she chose some earlier time like the dinosaur age. But there had been no humans then, just creatures that became some sort of chimp then her human ancestor, on her mother's side, of course, not Kald's. The idea of going back in time to rub out Jimmy Wright's ancestors was appealing despite Sci-Fi movies warning that fiddling with the past mucked up the future.

'Can you see the bad men?' whispered Poss.

'What?' said Viv then realised she must look grim. 'I was thinking of something else,' she said, and forced a smile. She wondered if Poss knew who the *bad men* were but did not want to dredge up the horror by asking.

'Let's have a little rest,' she said instead and plonked down on a stone. The sun was setting to her left which meant they travelled north *if* it worked the same here as at home but if Poss's home *were* north, why had her *da* taken her south to an *unsafe* settlement? Unless he was among the dead, although the way Poss spoke did not suggest it.

Poss watched her and when Viv tentatively opened her arms, Poss scrambled onto her lap and burrowed down, her need for comfort greater than her fear. It had been the same need that had kept Viv in Jimmy Wright's violence-filled house.

No child should have to live in fear, she thought angrily, surprised by the surge of protectiveness. It must be instinct, she concluded dryly, like the alley cats with litters that stood their ground against the gang's steel-capped boots, but for the first time since learning she was infertile, she felt something other than relief.

138

Chapter 26

It was dark before they reached the top and Viv shivered in a chill wind. She still wore her shirt halter-neck style and thanks to Poss's shoe, it was a lot shorter. But she would have been cold anyway. The ridgetop was exposed and the other side too steep to risk in the dark, especially with a child. 'Da waits for the zadic,' said Poss beside her.

Viv had no idea what a *zadic* was or how soon it would arrive. 'Are ... are there caves nearby?' she asked as her shivering grew.

'No. Da makes a fire.'

Let us hear it for *da*, thought Viv bad-temperedly. No doubt he was handy with flints or matches or whatever else these people used. There seemed to be bushes down slope but it was hard to tell, the stars a hell of lot duller than yesterday's. 'We need t-to get out of the w-wind,' she said and took Poss's hand.

Her hand was cold and Viv tightened her grip as she picked her way down. The blotches *were* bushes and there were stands of dry grass nearby which meant she could make a nest. 'We graze the urrut here in early Pool but the grass is too dry now,' said Poss.

'It will be warm though,' said Viv, too chilled to worry about what *early pool* and *urrut* were. She pushed her way into the bushes, trying not to think of bloat-bellied spiders, and was pleased by how much warmer it was.

'Da brings a maark to sleep under,' said Poss.

'This will be more fun,' said Viv pulling up clumps of grass. Shit! It was like telling some homeless person a cardboard box was jollier than blankets. 'Do you want to p— go to the toilet before we snuggle down?'

'*Torlett*?'

'You know, pee, relieve yourself …' Viv trailed off at Poss's expression.

'*Quarash* is private,' the child said huffily.

Add *quarash* to the list of things you know stuff-all about, Viv told herself. 'Lie down then,' she said, and when Poss had done so, Viv lay down behind her to shelter her and pulled a layer of grass over them both. Poss warmed but Viv's back was icy. *What a surprise, Vivi. Dry grass just ain't doin' it.*

Viv ignored Rim's intrusion, her thoughts on the delicious warmth her wings would provide if she wrapped them over but the risk was too great, even after Poss slept. The murderers who destroyed the settlements might be near and there was nothing to say Poss's people were not witch-burners. All she could do was change her shirt so it covered her back and revert to the halter-neck style tomorrow after *quarash*.

'Tell me about *Sindarella*,' said Poss sleepily.

'Ah, the girl with one shoe,' said Viv and chose the version that came from great, great, grandma Rose. It was older than Disney's with its pumpkin coach and fairy godmother. In the tale Lettie told her, a tree had grown out of the mother's grave, and it was this tree, nourished by the dead mother's love for her daughter, that provided Cinderella with a hiding place and the magic she needed to escape her miserable life.

Viv had cherished the story after her mother's disappearance, not just because the trees at the back of the house provided Viv with hiding places, but because Viv imagined her mother's love lived on after death too.

But Viv was only a little way into the story when Poss interrupted to ask what *grave* was and seemed even more

140

confused after Viv's explanation. 'But if the ground is on top of Sindarella's mother, how can her amé guide her to the stars?' she asked.

'It's an old story from a place a long way from here,' said Viv, worrying about transference again. She still wore the bracelet from the birdman's fold under her sleeve, although it would not be transference *if* she were still in the same fold, but the bindings on Poss's foot certainly were *and* Poss's memories of her when Viv had transited. She pressed on with the story, leaving out the gorier parts where the ugly sisters had cut their feet to fit the shoe.

'Why didn't Sindarella choose a father who would look after her better?' asked Poss.

'What—' began Viv and gasped as someone shone a flashlight full in her face.

'The Pool Zadic,' mumbled Poss, snuggling closer.

Viv stared up in astonishment. The sky was afire with a constellation that stretched across the heavens like an undulating wave. It illuminated Poss's sleepy face and the patterning on her clothes. They were another variation of the straight and wavy lines and confirmed Viv *had* transited *within* the fold and that meant Thris and Ky might have too.

She fought the urge to leap up and go in search of them. She had pledged to take Poss to safety, she reminded herself, although no one knew of the pledge. The Principae probably did, she countered and *she* knew. There was only one more ridge between them and safety anyway. One more ridge and then she would be free to search for Thris.

Dawn revealed the next ridge soared high above them and Viv's heart sank. It would take at least a day to climb and that was after they reached the valley floor. Poss would slow her too, for without food, the little girl would weaken unless Viv found some of the mysterious blackbor.

Poss still slept and Viv roused her, eager to be gone. 'Is there water nearby?' she asked, as Poss rubbed her face.

'Eye-Serier,' the little girl mumbled.

'Is that far?' Poss pointed up at a cave on the next ridge. 'Is there any of that *blackbor* near here?' pursued Viv.

'It's at Eye-Serier.'

'Eye-Serier it is then,' said Viv. They set off but Poss was even slower than Viv feared and the descent too steep to carry her. Viv was glad she had not tackled it in the dark although it might have been doable once the *Pool Zadic* had appeared. Viv knew little about astronomy but constellations did not just pop into the sky or at least not in Moonsun.

Your fold has a moon and a sun, hence the name, Thris had explained, early in her time in Ezam. Her old life in Australia seemed years ago now but Viv had no idea how long it really was. According to Thris, no time had elapsed in Moonsun since she left but what of Ezam? It had been even harder to gauge time there and what of this fold, the fold *she could not seem leave*?

Thris said a fold with a rift in, had a rift out but what if the rift *out* delivered you back *in*? Her head swam. Being marooned here for years could mean just a couple of seconds in Ezam and by the time Thris returned, she might be decrepit or long dead. Viv struggled not to panic. There had been a rift in the cave where she found

142

Poss and one on the cliff face Thris *might* have used to escape the monkey-dwarf attack. So, that made two rifts at least, plus the water rift, which had boomeranged her into the same fold but might exit elsewhere next time.

If worse came to worse, she could fly back to where she found Poss or to the site of the monkey-dwarf attack. Finding either again was a longshot, a voice in her head cautioned, but it gave her hope.

Viv descended slowly but had to stop regularly for Poss to catch up which gave her plenty of time to wonder whether Thris were still nearby. 'Can you walk any faster?' she asked when Poss came level.

'I'm tired.'

'I'll carry you,' said Viv, and scooped her up. 'You can have a little rest at the bottom. There might be some water there as well as blackbor.'

'There's no water at Serier,' said Poss.

'There might be,' said Viv.

Poss just lay her head on Viv's shoulder and Viv struggled on. It was awkward carrying Poss downslope and the birds that burst from the bushes she passed put her on edge. 'Leaf-lilters,' said Poss. 'They eat the scharii.'

They reached the bottom of the slope and Viv set Poss down and sleeved the sweat from her face. There was no water and Viv kicked at the ground in disgust. 'What kind of fold has valleys with no streams?' she demanded in frustration.

'There's water at Eye-Serier,' said Poss dully.

Viv looked at her closely. 'Are you *very* thirsty?'

'Da says talking about thirst makes it worse.' The child's grubby hands gripped each other as if seeking comfort and Viv's anger at Poss's father grew. He was starting to sound like some sort of boot-camp commando; a man big on bluster but not on action, given Poss had been left to fend for herself.

Viv's hands came to her hips as she stared about. The valley would have made a pleasant picnic spot had there been bushes laden with berries or nuts and a stream but instead it was just a place that risked attack. Even as the thought crossed her mind, birds took flight from the next ridge.

'Ridge-roosters are fidget birds,' said Poss. 'Da says even a moss-mouse will scatter them.' Or a murdering thug, thought Viv. The birds settled again and she picked up Poss and started up the slope. It was a harder climb than the last one and she was considering how long they would rest at the cave when the stench hit her. She hoped the stink was a dead bird putrefying in the sun but as they drew closer, the smell of human excrement was unmistakable. 'The bad men,' whispered Poss and buried her head in Viv's shoulder.

At least there was water, a trickle from the cave's side, but Viv worried it had been fouled. 'I need to check the water's clean,' she said but Poss clung like a limpet and Viv was forced to take her inside. Excrement had been smeared around the walls and its carvings smashed like the other cave.

Poss whimpered and Viv gave up on her plan to search for false backs and rifts, just made sure the stream was clear before she picked her way outside. Poss immediately wriggled from of her arms, completed her pre-drink ritual, and guzzled the water down. Viv sat on the stone and watched her. It would be dark before they reached the summit, which was convenient for anyone who planned an ambush, but then a worse thought occurred to her. If the thugs who had wiped out the settlements and despoiled the caves headed north too, they might be just ahead! Or they might have finished their murderous jaunt and be on the way south again, *or* Poss's people might even be driving them south!

'Aren't you going to drink?' asked Poss.

Viv shook her head, distracted by the possibility of coming face to face with a pack of murdering thugs. 'We need to keep moving. It'll be dark soon.'

'There's a path the rest of the way,' said Poss. Viv's hopes rose but Poss's path turned out to be only slightly smoother patches between the rocks. It still allowed faster travel and they reached the ridgetop as dusk settled over the lands.

Viv stopped to draw breath and then swore as she realised she had forgotten to search for blackbor at the cave. It would not matter if Poss's home were close but there were no signs of any settlement. She peered down the ridge's northern slope. It was gentle and thick with trees. They would make good shelter but Viv feared what they might hide.

A breeze rustled their leaves and Poss clutched her hand. 'What is it?' whispered Viv and then the acrid smell of burned earth reached her too. 'Poss,' she said gently, but Poss abruptly wrenched her hand free. The bracelet had slid down Viv's wrist and Poss stared at it in terror. 'Waradi,' she gasped and fled.

Chapter 27

Thris exited Haven and powered away to the Blue Helixai, angled up sharply to land at Ash's favourite cavern, and stared at the lands below as he bedded his wings. His skin gleamed under Ezam's umber sky and his violet eyes were intent. He might look the same to those who knew him as just another Dane but to those who *really* knew him, he was utterly changed.

Prime-archae Serith had chanced upon him earlier under the glis. 'He is transformed,' he told Mirek, but had said little else and Mirek was eager to discuss Thrisdane's new state with Ashdane, but the blue angel had disappeared.

Thris knew Ash's love for the Blue Helixai's brooding solitude was the most likely reason for his long absence and ignorance of Thris's return and Ky's injuries. Ky had woken dazed and terrified, and while his confusion had dissipated, he remained convinced the Dendrinai harboured unspeakable threats. Thris had left him under Haven's portico, surrounded by the friendly chatter of Dane, but was in a hurry to return. Caring for Ky meant he had yet to visit Archae Kald who would be rightly angered Thris had failed the Guideship. a second time, but choosing between Ky's welfare and the shekinah's had left Thris torn in two.

Even now, after so many cycles, thoughts of the shekinah brought his wings erect and triggered an ache in his body that brought him to his knees. He stared at the blue stone dazedly and when awareness finally returned, was alarmed by how much time he sensed had passed.

He swiftly harmonised and given his violations, was mystified by how easily he came into alignment *and* by the acuity of his senses. Joining with the shekinah had gifted him a sensitivity shockingly at odds with the perverseness of the act and he wondered whether such sensitivity was the preserve of the Archae. Perhaps the Great Beyond kept the Host separate from the Iahhel to prevent angels *stealing* a state that must be earned. Perhaps it was the *struggle* to ascend that allowed entry to the Great Beyond not a particular achievement.

It would explain the white in Ash's wings, and— Thris sucked in his breath and brought his wings forward. There was no white in his and he bowed his head. It had been madness to imagine that despite his transgressions he would ever ascend and that madness had passed.

Erasing all hope from his mind, he turned back to the cavern. Its shadowed depths yawned before him but what held him motionless at the entrance was the understanding Ash was not within, in fact, had not been there for many cycles. A flash of white caught his eye and he turned to see the White Helixai shining in the distance.

Ash loved the Blue but he was at the White. Thris had no idea where the certainty sprang from only that it was there. Delaying no longer, he launched from the ledge and flew in its direction.

Thris had not visited the White Helixai since being new to Ezam and had to circle its peak several times to find a place to land. It gave him plenty of time to examine it and what he saw was at odds with his memories. He remembered the Helixai as a white version of the Blue but it resembled the Quartz Stele more than a mountain with a mix of translucent, milky, and smoky stone.

Thris stilled his wings but did not bed them. There had been mist in the fold where the shekinah had been lost to him and as he directed his senses into the White Helixai, the stone gave way as the mist had, but at an enormous cost. He was trembling with exhaustion before he sensed Ash's resonance and then horror overtook him. Ash's resonance was static *as if he were dead.*

Ky huddled on the portico step and hugged himself as if Ezam's mild air had chilled. The Dane nearby engaged in light-hearted debates or bragged about their chances in the next round of trials but he felt utterly alone. The glis pressed in just beyond Haven's white marble, its murk reminiscent of what had hidden the murderous long-armed creatures. A part of him knew he was safe in Ezam but it made no difference.

A grey-skinned Dane gave him a friendly grin but Ky was incapable of responding and shame at his rudeness added to his distress. Even the dangerous glis seemed preferable to insulting his fellow Dane and he struggled upright and tottered down the portico's steps .He would not go far, just somewhere quiet to curl up and wait for Thris, but then a blue-robed angel appeared.

Archae Kald was unaware of his proximity to Haven having been distracted by his encounter with the Quartz Stele. The stele was a powerful amplifier of spiritual energy but instead of aiding his meditations, it had filled his head with jumbled thoughts of his shekinah, his protégé, and Dejon's protégé. Resonance intruded and Kald's sharp gaze took in Kydane. 'Where is Thrisdane?' he demanded.

'I do not know, Archae, but he will be back soon.'

'He located the shekinah and brought her back under his care?'

'Yes, Archae.'

'And received my instructions to return her here?'

'Yes, Archae.'

Kald's tension eased. 'Your role of Shadow requires that you remain with Thrisdane. Why have you separated?'

'I . . . I was injured, Archae. There . . . there are terrible things in the folds. They . . . '

Kydane had obviously abandoned his responsibilities and fled and Kald's sense of well-being intensified as he calculated the cost to his rival. 'Does your mentor know of your return?' he asked.

The Dane dropped his head. 'No, Archae, I—'

Kald smiled. 'I am sure he will be *delighted* by the news,' he said and sauntered on.

Chapter 28

Poss bolted down the slope with Viv in hot pursuit. 'Poss,' she shouted. 'I'm not Waradi! I won't hurt you! Poss!' Her ruckus told every murdering bastard within miles of their presence but Poss had disappeared into the trees *where the smell of burning* had come from.

It was completely dark under the canopy and silent which meant Poss had gone to ground. 'Poss,' she shouted again. 'I *found* the bracelet. I don't own it. I'm not Waradi!' Nothing. Shit! Shit! Shit! Maybe Poss had simply run home, in which case da might be readying his gun. *Best get ya arse outa there, Vivi.* But given the smell of burning, Viv suspected there was *no* home to run to or even worse, no da. The last thing she wanted was for Poss to find da's charred and mutilated corpse.

Spread ya wings an' flap away, Vivi. The brat's probably got folks nearby, but even if she ain't, motherhood's ain't ya gig. Ya going to have to leave her one day or give up travellin' the rifts. Ya can't take her with you.

But Viv could not simply abandon a child. The smell of burning intensified as she went on and then the trees gave way to a charred clearing and she stopped. The starlight revealed the curved walls of a blackened building, broken timbers, and shards of pottery and glass. The destruction looked old except for a gob of fire, the contents of a broken oil pot perhaps, that still burned.

There was *something* beside it, a wavering, wraith-like figure, and Viv shivered as she recalled the gangs' claims that ghosts escaped through the mouths of dead junkies.

It was Poss, she realised in relief, her small frame illuminated by the flickering flame.

'Poss,' she cried but as she started forward, something moved at the edge of her vision. She ducked instinctively but the blow knocked her to the ground. The world rocked sickeningly but she managed to raise her head and then a second blow sent her crashing into oblivion.

Viv stared up into Thris's glorious face, his scent dusting down on her as his strong, cool arms cradled her close. Her heart sang but she knew it was a dream and knowing meant the dream already slipped away. Viv fought to hold onto it, to hold onto Thris, but it went the way of all dreams and the world returned, bringing with it music, the smell of a fire, and a sickening head ache.

She groaned, the music stopped, and she was hauled into a sitting position, sagged sideways, and was wrenched upright again. Poss sat opposite, beyond the fire, with a bowl of food in her lap. 'Poss,' croaked Viv. 'I'm not going to hurt you.'

'*That* at least is true,' said a male voice, 'unlike the rest of the lies you've told her.'

'I don't lie,' mumbled Viv automatically, as she struggled to focus on her captor. Beads flashed in his braided hair and his jacket shone with metallic thread. He looked like some sort of drag-queen, she thought dully. 'Is this your da?' she asked Poss, then realised the idea was ludicrous. Apart from their physical differences, Poss's clothes were of natural fibres and dyes and her captor's like a peacock's.

'I'm not so favoured,' said the man. 'What's more relevant is what a Waradi wants with an Eshadi child.'

151

'I'm not Waradi,' said Viv.

The flame caught the polished metal as the man dangled the bracelet in front of her. 'You're lein-trysted to one so it's the same thing. I repeat, what do you want with an Eshadi child?'

The man had knocked her out rather than killed her and Poss did not seem afraid of him *and* he played music. Her fear eased a little but then Rim's sarcastic voice intruded. *So, no murderer's ever been musical, eh Vivi?*

'What do *you* want with her?' she countered. The man smiled in a way that made her shiver. He might look like drag-queen but he was not averse to dishing out pain. 'Poss probably told you I found her hiding in a cave. I just want to deliver her to her family and be on my way.'

'Why would a Waradi want to do that?'

'I'm not a Waradi,' she repeated. The man held the bracelet up again and this time his smile was mocking. 'It's as I've told Poss,' said Viv. 'I found it.'

'*Found* a tryst-bracelet? Where? In your Waradi lover's bed?'

Viv struggled to think. If the cock-fighters were this man's mates, he would be angry she had ruined their gaming but surely the punishment was not to be death? And while she argued with this *drag-queen*, the arseholes who murdered and burned might be closing in.

'I found the bracelet in a cage,' said Viv reluctantly. 'It was being used to make some birdman creatures fight. Men were taking bets on the outcome. It was cruel. I . . . I took the bracelet to stop the fight.'

She half expected the man to roar with laughter or strike her but he simply stared. 'That's so unlikely it might actually be true,' he said. 'Why were you in the Leferen?'

'I was looking for my mother.'

His eyes bored into hers, but Viv found it easy to meet his gaze. For once she had not been forced to fudge the truth. He slipped the bracelet into his pocket, settled beside Poss on the other side of the fire, and resumed his own meal.

'She's hungry too,' said Poss, her dark eyes on Viv.

'She can wait,' the man said.

He obviously intended to starve her into submission and Viv toyed with the idea of playing hungry and desperate, but the charade would waste time and she needed to get Poss away. At least Poss was at ease in the man's company which meant she probably knew him, *and* he had given her food. His animosity seemed to stem from his belief that, as a Waradi, Viv meant Poss harm. If she could convince him she was not the enemy, he might help her but if not, he might kill her.

Chapter 29

Viv tried to harmonise but being bound made it impossible. If only she had not kept that bloody bracelet. She had hung onto it even after guessing she was in the same fold and that tossing it down some rabbit hole would not have been transference but Viv had never owned anything beautiful before.

First rule of the gangs, Vivi. What's yours is ours, so best keep what's yours to a minimum, eh? Rim had smiled smarmily but she had already learned that lesson from Jimmy Wright. Memories of the drunken thug added to the throb in her head and Poss's distrust tore at her too. 'I'd never hurt you, Poss,' she whispered.

'Her name's not *Poss*,' the man said, taking a swig from his water bottle.

'Well, as you obviously know her name and where her family is, take her to them,' said Viv angrily. 'It's too dangerous here.'

'What makes you think so?'

'This,' she said, nodding at the wreckage, 'is hardly the work of friends. They burned the settlement two ridges back too and killed those there. The cave where I found Poss was full of their crap. So was Eye - something or other, just over that ridge. I know you don't trust me but at least take Poss to safety!'

'What do you think?' the man asked, turning to Poss. 'Should we trust Viv and do as she says?' Poss dropped her head and the man smiled. 'A wise child,' he murmured.

'A child who's seen terrible things,' retorted Viv. 'A child who's had to hide in a hole in a shit-filled cave. A child who needs to be safe with those who love her!'

The man made no reply but the sneer left his face. He finished his meal and busied himself setting a shelter akin to a two-man tent and when he finished, Poss crawled inside. He crouched at its entrance and they exchanged soft words, then he collected firewood from among the debris. The chill air added to Viv's discomfort but as she shuffled closer to the fire, a knife thumped into the ground near her thigh.

'Just a little reminder that *I'll* decide when you depart,' he said as he reclaimed it.

Viv bit back a retort and as the warmth eased her muscles, made another *successful* attempt to harmonise and the ache in her head faded. The Pool Zadic ignited in the sky and Viv took a deep breath as she stared up at it.

'Viv's a peculiar name,' the man's voice intruded. He was back in the wreckage, collecting more firewood.

'At least I have a name,' she said, keeping her gaze on the stars.

The man laughed. 'I am named Tarchen en-Scharii. Forgive my lack of courtesy,' he added ironically.

'I won't be forgiving anything until you untie my hands.'

'Then I must remain unforgiven, at least until you tell the truth.'

His footsteps paused behind her and Viv's alignment slipped. 'I've told you no lies,' she said hurriedly.

'En-valen?'

'I don't come from the Vales.'

'There's nowhere else.' Poss said their dead journeyed to the stars but she kept her mouth shut. It was not worth

155

the risk to suggest she came from *beyond* his world, not when he might be a witch-burner. 'You admire the Pool Zadic, I see,' he said. 'It's beautiful but surely less so than the undulations of the Horse Zadic?'

Viv recalled the spectacular red, yellow, and green stars of the cat creature's fold *and* its ferocious inhabitants. 'All stars are beautiful,' she muttered.

'You need to drink,' he said abruptly and fetching his water bottle, crouched in front of her. Viv shook her head, wanting him away. 'You didn't drink at Eye-Serier either,' he said softly, 'despite carrying the child a good way up the ridge. It's not an easy climb and even after being carried by you, the child was thirsty and yet you were not.'

The Zadic's light showed the hard planes of his face and Viv looked away but he caught her chin and turned her face back to his. 'Our music carries us on journeys through settlements where urrut number in their hundreds and through far flung vals where Valen prefer their own company and ways. No crest impedes the Scharii, no roaring cade turns us aside. The Argine and the Lefer receive our music, and the wild folk in the misted forests sing with us in their harsh voices, and yet . . .'

His thumb caressed the soft hollow under her eye. 'And yet, in all my travels, never have I seen one such as you. Never such eyes, never such hair, never such perfection.' Viv's heart pounded and his hand caught the back of her neck and jerked her close. 'I—know— what—you—are!'

He slammed her to the ground and Viv twisted her head in time to see a knife catch the firelight then felt it slice the back of her neck. Blood oozed down her shirt and she was too shocked to resist as he rolled her over and bound her ankles. 'A little test,' he said thickly. 'We shall see what the morrow brings.'

Thris's wings thrashed as he fought to impose order on his thoughts. If Ash were dead . . . He could get no further, the future impossible to imagine without his friend. He managed to still his wings but the impulse to rush into the cavern was harder to quell. If the White Helixai were like the Blue and trapped him, there would be no rescue for either of them.

Thris trembled as competing demands tore at him. He had abandoned the shekinah in a hostile fold and Ky to his fear. Was he to desert the other being who gave meaning to his life? Angels were not immortal but death was rare in Ezam and while angels might linger for millennia uncounted, in the end, they all stumbled upon a path that delivered them to the Great Beyond.

Thris sent his senses coursing back into the mountain and a tart vapour erupted from his skin then he sagged panting against the stone. Ash was not dead but his resonance was curiously congealed, reminding Thris of a time he had exited a rift into Moonsun's snow-covered mountains and come across a frozen pool. Its aqua had been reminiscent of the Principae's glory and there had been a Moonsun butterfly suspended in the ice. He had chipped it free but as the ice had melted, it had collapsed broken onto the snow. It had been blue, like Ash, and he wondered if the memory were a warning against a rescue attempt.

It was Ash who usually did the rescuing, concluded Thris and faltered as he perceived a pattern. Being trapped in the Blue Helixai's tunnels and torn apart in

Beast Fold had forced Ash to develop the skills to save him, as had Ky being all but suffocated in Sand Fold. And while it was he and Ky who obeyed their mentors' instructions to transit the rifts, journeys intended to elevate them to Quin-archae, it was Ash's wings that displayed the white plumage of ascension.

The insight filled Thris with joy but did not resolve whether Ash *chose* to remain in the White Helixai or was imprisoned there. Ash's long absence suggested the latter but Thris was troubled by the memory of the broken butterfly.

He paced up and down the ledge then stared down at the Dendrinai, home to the pristine marble of the Halls and Haven and the darker stone of the Bokos, the repository of angel lore and the haunt of the only senior angel Ash *trusted*.

Chapter 30

Mirek now spent almost as much time at the Bokos as Serith, studying near a window so that glimpses of lacewings or sumi compensated him for the shadowy spaces he endured. His studies revealed how limited Ezam's castes were compared to other folds although perhaps limited was not the right word, he decided, for it suggested a lack and Ezam lacked nothing. Rather it seemed that Ezam's castes were gloriously simple.

Serith's resonance intruded and Mirek smiled. For a time after Serith's testing by the Black Obsidian Stele, Mirek feared he had lost his friend and in a sense, he had; the silver-haired angel who now appeared very different to the one who had sought the daimon's destruction.

Mirek did not greet him until Serith's face registered recognition, his introspection one of the changes many students of the Bokos found insulting. Serith often seemed unaware of others, wandered off in mid conversation, and said things that bore no relation to what was discussed. Had they listened, the scholars might have learned what eons of study had yet to gift them, but they were too affronted.

Serith settled at the table and Mirek fetched a jug of ambrosia and two goblets. 'The blue angel,' began Serith, without any preamble.

'Do you know where he is?' asked Mirek eagerly.

'He has passed into the Great Beyond.'

Mirek's hand jerked, splashing ambrosia over his robe. 'Ashdane has transcended?' he gasped.

'Senquar-archae.'

'Oh,' said Mirek and felt a surge of sympathy for those who shunned Serith. He brushed himself down, topped up his goblet and drank. 'Have you learned more of Senquar-archae?'

'I have learned more of the Helixai.'

'But not of Senquar-archae?' pursued Mirek.

'All things in Ezam are connected,' said Serith tranquilly.

Mirek had never considered himself impatient but he quelled an impulse to shake his friend, more worried about Ashdane than he cared to admit. He took a gulp of ambrosia and distracted himself with the view from the window. A mantise swayed, bright against the silvery glis, seized a scarab, and devoured it.

'Without mantises Ezam would be overwhelmed by scarabs, and without scarabs, choked by leaf-fall,' murmured Serith, following his gaze. 'All things in Ezam are connected,' he repeated, and smiled beatifically.

Mirek's heart quickened. 'Including the Helixai? What is it you have read?'

'The words of Senquar-archae himself.'

Mirek leaned forward expectantly but Serith's gaze remained on the mantise. Silence stretched and then Serith spoke so suddenly Mirek jumped. *Light is the lure and light the trap, light the maze and light the map. The red, the blue, and the white don't show, what mantise, scarab and sumi know.*

His words were strangely rhythmic. 'Is it a song?' asked Mirek curiously. He had read Moonsun human caste stretched or compressed words to fit the resonance they called music. The list of colours surely alluded to the Helixai, except the Green was missing, but he could make no sense of the rest of it. Senquar-archae's words were unangelic, he concluded in frustration. It was human caste who twisted meaning, not the Host.

'I think Senquar-archae intended to be unclear,' said Serith.

'Well he succeeded,' grumbled Mirek.

'I think he intended to be unclear to warn or inform,' continued Serith, as if Mirek had not spoken. 'The Host claims to search for a truth that will deliver us from Ezam and yet spurns the steles and Helixai. Does that not seem odd to you, Mirek?'

'I think some of the Host are more limited than they believe,' said Mirek uncomfortably.

'And some of the Host more advanced than they believe,' said Serith.

Mirek had the peculiar sensation he was in the presence of a stele, as if Serith probed him in some way, and he took another gulp of ambrosia and smoothed his damp robe. 'I wonder—' he began, but at that moment Prime-archae Jaril approached, his arms loaded with scrolls.

'A Dane requests speech with you,' he said, and beckoned an angel forward.

Mirek's hopes rose but the angel that stepped from the shadows was Thrisdane. He carried his immense black wings exposed and their plumage ran with green-blue fire in the window's light. The same light glanced off the gleaming planes of his body, exquisite in their perfection, and Mirek recalled Serith's description of him as *transformed*.

Thrisdane palmed and straightened. 'Prime-archae Mirek,' he said. 'Ash is trapped in the White Helixai and I do not know what to do.'

161

Ky remained huddled in the glis, long after Archae Kald had gone, the Archae's words having brought home to him the full depth of his appalling failures. He had failed the Principaes' trust, his mentor's trust, and Thris's trust, and every challenge in the folds. He had fled the human caste in Hearth Fold, stood uselessly by while Thris was attacked in Beast Fold, and all but suffocated in Sand Fold.

Fear had taken root in him like some vile human caste disease and grown until it controlled his every thought and action. *Fear* had compelled him to travel with Thris when his duties demanded he stay apart and *fear* had forced Thris to rescue him when the Guideship demanded Thris stay with the shekinah.

Archae Kald would be furious when he learned Thris had returned without her, as would his own mentor whose orders, to ensure Thris brought the shekinah back, had been explicit. Ky stared blank-eyed at his surroundings. Ezam was beautiful but its promise of ascension was lost to him now, all because of the shekinah.

It was *her* filthy human caste traits that had destroyed everything he held dear: the Guideship, his role as Shadow, and Thris, his glorious flesh undone by hers. Fury mounted, an emotion so alien, he had no idea what possessed him. He slapped at his body but the boiling throb grew until he bolted as if he could outrun it.

On and on he fled through the glis until its metallic leaves turned red and then the power of what drove him trebled. Somewhere beyond his pounding blood, he was aware of the Red Jade Stele, but his awareness was fleeting. Caught in the stele's thrall, he stormed around it in ever decreasing circles, tearing at the glis and vines.

Hate mixed with anger, its corrosive scald so powerful, he threw his head back and howled.

Deep in the White Helixai, Ash roused, but it was Thris who exploded into action. A single bound took him out of the Bokos's window into the air and he streaked over the Dendrinai and was almost to the Red Jade Stele when Ky burst from the canopy. Thris vaned back his wings as he too was caught in the Red Jade's net, but while the stele multiplied Ky's anger and hate, it amplified Thris's love for his friend.

Ky crashed back through the glis and Thris followed needing to calm Ky before he injured himself but Ky was lost in a maelstrom of fury. Thris judged his moment and lunged, fastening his arms around Ky's shoulders but Ky broke free with a burst of manic strength. Thris resisted the urge to tackle him again, instead he flew up through the break in the canopy and hovered.

He heard wood smash and splinter below but clenched his jaw and waited, and his patience was rewarded when Ky rocketed up through the glis. Thris seized him, pinned Ky's wings flat with his body, and wrenched him clear. Ky fought but Thris held him in an iron grip and bore him away.

Haven held nothing to cure Ky's malaise and Thris coursed for steles. He sensed the Ametrine Stele but flew on until the vibration of the Carnelian reached him. Some angels went for eons without encountering steles but not Thris who considered himself blessed. The steles held extraordinary power and while they could be brutal, as the Red Jade and Black Obsidian were, they could also be healing, as the Carnelian was.

Ky had quietened but grew agitated again as the glis leaves reddened in the stele's glow. 'It is the *Carnelian*

Stele not the Red Jade,' Thris reassured him, as he came into land. Ky seemed to relax but then he drove his elbow into Thris's stomach, broke free, and fled through the trees. Thris staggered after him and by the time he had picked up speed, Ky had disappeared. His resonance was clear though as was the resonant print of a rift.

Thris pushed himself to greater speed but while his body worked with machine precision, his mind had dissolved into chaos. Ash trapped in the White Helixai, Archae Kald awaiting his report, the shekinah lost in the folds. Who was he to abandon this time? Citrus fumed from his skin that had nothing to do with exertion and when Ky's resonance suddenly ceased, Thris gave an agonised cry, and ran headlong into the rift after him.

Chapter 31

I know what you are; the drag-queen's words beat like a drum in Viv's brain. He had cut her to see how quickly she healed and the wound had already lost its throb. Perhaps if she managed to reopen it . . . but it would make no difference. *I know what you are.*

The temperature dropped and Viv would have frozen had it not been for the fire. *Ya going to lie there like some effing lamb to the slaughter, Vivi? Get ya arse into gear.* Rim's contemptuous voice penetrated her daze and she managed to sit up. The drag-queen slept; if she were going to save her skin, it had to be now.

Trussed up victims in movies cut their bonds with something sharp, but in real life, it was a hell of a lot harder. There were shards of glass and crockery in the debris but she had to find a useful bit first, manoeuvre it behind her back, and somehow use it like a knife.

The drag-queen's pack was propped against the shelter and while she bet he owned more than one knife, she also bet he was a light sleeper. Even so, his pack was her best option and she shuffled towards it on her backside and had covered half the distance when something whirred overhead. Viv cringed, expecting a knife in the back, but the sound belonged to an owl, now perched on a branch above the shelter.

She had loved the barn owl's heart-shaped face and the boobooks' haunting calls at home but mythic owls were often fey and Viv was still wondering whether *this* owl was a good or bad omen when it took flight *in the opposite direction*. Viv stared around, heart pounding.

The firelight barely reached the ruined buildings and the forest was full of furtive shufflings.

She searched the darkness, fearful she was about to be carried off like a convenience food, trussed up and ready to go, and saw movement. She watched in horrified fascination as whatever it was drew inexorably closer and saw in relief it was another drag-queen.

He closed the last of distance quickly, his gaze darting between her, the ruined buildings, and the shelter. He carried a pack with a shield slung over the top, and while his hair was darker than Tarchen's, they looked similar enough to be brothers.

He stopped in front of the shelter, dropped his pack and shield to the ground, and barked Tarchen's name. Tarchen appeared looking dishevelled and what followed was a verbal brawl. The new comer was obviously in charge but Tarchen was far from cowed. They argued in a strange tongue but Tarchen's meaning was clear when he strode to Viv, shoved her head down, and exposed the cut to her neck.

Silence followed and Viv heard Poss begin to cry. 'If you're going to kill me, do it somewhere else,' she muttered. 'Poss has seen enough death.'

The new comer growled an order and Tarchen released her and then he crouched in front of her instead. 'The Scharii practice the ways of music not of death,' he said, his gaze on her unwavering despite another tirade from Tarchen.

'Don't just leave her to cry,' snapped Viv, as Poss's sobbing grew. 'She's frightened.'

The new comer issued another command and with a final glare, Tarchen ducked back into the shelter.

166

'Tarchen tells me you're an Astraali who warms a Waradi's bed,' the new comer said.

'Tarchen's wrong.'

'On all counts? Consider well before you answer. We aid neither Waradi against Eshadi, nor Eshadi against Ascadi. Our concern is with music, not with the brawls of Sylds, but we will punish those whose *discord* disturbs our harmonies.'

'I'm not Astraali and I have nothing to do with the Waradi.'

Viv cringed as the man unsheathed his knife but he simply cut her bindings and tossed the cords into the fire. Pain throbbed through her cramped muscles and Viv rolled her shoulders as the man rebuilt the fire and set a pot of water on the coals.

Poss had stopped crying and Viv glanced uneasily at the tent. 'The Scharii do not harm children,' said the man, following her gaze. 'The gift of music is purest in the young.'

It did not seem like a very good reason but Viv was grateful for anything that kept Poss safe. When the water boiled, he tossed in leaves from a pouch in his pack and a liquorice smell filled the air. A second pouch revealed a slab of something dark and sticky and he cut off a portion and offered it to her. 'I am Darch en-Scharii,' he said formally. 'Please accept my food.'

It seemed like some sort of apology and Viv took the sticky substance, sniffed it, and took a careful bite. It tasted like dried figs and dates and was very sweet. She was hungry, as she always was after injury, but she mainly ate to avoid offending Darch. He seemed more rational than Tarchen but wore knives at his belt like his fairer version. Both men would have been a good fit for the gangs, except for their clothes. Rim hated *effing queers*.

'When was the last time you ate?' asked Darch.

Darch's interrogation had begun and Viv tossed up between remaining silent and answering, cursing again that lying was not an option. She searched her memory. 'In Ezam, I think,' she said.

'*When* not where.'

'I don't know,' said Viv. She had no idea how time was measured here or how it compared to Sand Fold or the cat creature's fold or Moth Fold, or to Ezam, for that matter.

'I gather you don't need to eat often, *like the Astraali*,' he said. 'Or drink, according to Tarchen, another *Astraali* trait. As is your hair, a rare colour in the Vales, though not unknown *when* combined with *brown* eyes. And your body's ability to heal . . .' he paused. 'I wager were I to cut every part of you, in a few days your skin would be as perfect as it is now.'

The food formed a lump in Viv's throat and Darch's voice softened. 'You have no need to fear the Scharii. The Valen don't love the Astraali and there are reasons why Tarchen shares their distaste but his methods of eliciting the truth are *discordant*. I express regret for them on behalf of the Scharii.'

It was a convoluted way of saying Tarchen was out of order but Darch did not seem a whole lot better, given he was unlikely to let her simply walk away. He retrieved silver cups from his pack, filled them from the pot, and handed her one. Viv found it incongruous that such fine objects were used for camping and she traced their engravings with her fingers: mountains, lakes, and forests, all arranged in circles.

'Recognise the design?' asked Darch. It reminded Viv of Ezam, but she kept her mouth shut.

'Astraal, crystal city of the Astraali, who once gifted their star-thoughts to the Valen but who do so no longer.' Darch paused. 'Their thoughts weren't all they gifted; they gifted their seed too.'

Viv's grip on the cup tightened. Darch obviously thought she was an Astraali bastard and given Tarchen's reaction, that was not good news.

'If you spoke truthfully to Tarchen, you have seen the Lefer, a creature with the thoughts of men locked in the body of birds. Some believe the Lefer are the result of Valen seeking mates amongst the *parien*, a bird no longer seen. The purity of each was lost and a lesser thing created. There was disharmony in the Vales until the Lefer made their home amongst the waste-wood.'

Viv had not been in a classroom since she was fourteen but she knew that while you could mate a donkey and a horse to get a mule, a man and a bird were too different to get anything. But all that seemed to matter to Darchen was purity and his belief that mixed parentage caused *disharmony*. He would get along just fine with Serith, she concluded sourly.

'No *Valen* would *choose* to have an Astraali father so that in the Vales, the unions remain hidden,' continued Darch, ' and if the child bears an Astraali face, they are raised in isolation and ignorance of their heritage. Things are different in the crystal city of Astraal where only the Scharii now bear witness to the *full* harmonic richness of The Wheel.'

Darch's face glowed with pride but Viv wondered how looking like an Astraali bastard would affect her time in the fold. Not well, she feared. Some musician's law might prevent Darch from killing her but probably no such laws restrained the rest of the Valen, and she was just considering it was lucky she had only come across a Valen child so far, when she remembered the man on the horse.

She had thought him intent on rape but now she wondered if her face and hair were to blame for his pursuit. Then again, he might not have even noticed her resemblance to the hated Astraali in the dark.

'Did your mother tell you who your seed-father was?' asked Darch.

'No.'

'And your choose-father? Did he know?'

Viv grappled with the concept of Jimmy Wright as a *choose*-father. Shit! Imagine his reaction to his beer money being squandered on another man's bastard, in fact, an effing *angel's* bastard. He would have killed Lettie *and* her.

Viv hugged herself as she wondered why Jimmy Wright had never suspected he had been duped. He had gingery hair and blue eyes, so she supposed she looked like him, which was lucky, unless … Viv faltered. *Unless it was why Lettie had married him*!

The bile rose in Viv's throat and the little in her stomach deposited itself on the grass as the reasons for her violence-filled childhood slammed home. Her mother had chosen Jimmy Wright as a husband to protect Viv but instead, had subjected them both to years of abuse.

Chapter 32

Darch waited in silence until Viv's stomach had quieted. 'I gather the answer to my last question is also *no*,' he said.

Viv was too distraught to reply. Why the hell had her mother not up and left? Why had she not been stronger? It was a different era, Viv reminded herself, but anger at her mother grew. And Viv was no better! She had put up with years of the gang's thuggery because anything was better than being alone.

The first of the birdsong echoed in the trees and Darch went back to the shelter and exchanged words with Tarchen but Viv ignored them. She felt empty, as if every surety had been stripped away. Her mother had trusted Kald and Kald had abandoned her. Her mother had sought shelter with Jimmy Wright, and Jimmy Wright had used her as a punching bag. Then Kald had turned up at Jimmy Wright's graveside and *Viv* had trusted him. Then the angel that Kald had trusted to protect her, had attacked her, and then on Kald's command, screwed her. Thris was not like Jimmy Wright or Kald, she argued, but the fact remained that when he had to choose between her and Ky, he had chosen Ky.

Poss came and settled beside her but Viv barely noticed. What was it about women that made them want to trust? To put themselves in men's power over and over again? What was it about *her*?

'I'm sorry I didn't trust you,' said Poss, in a small voice. 'I wanted to.'

'You were right not to,' said Viv grimly. 'You should never trust *anybody*.'

171

'That's what da says.'

'Your da is right.'

Darch offered her food but she shook her head, unable to choke it down. Poss ate, and Tarchen, and then they packed up their gear. Viv did not move. She had no food for Poss, no warm clothing, and no idea of the way ahead, all because she had trusted Thris, and now Poss wanted to trust *her*!

She would be doing Poss a big favour if she simply walked away or better still, if Darch and Tarchen took Poss with them. *They* knew the Vales; they might even know where Poss's surviving family were, *if* there were any. Viv clambered to her feet and went to where Darch readied his pack, careful to keep her voice low as she made the request but Darch made no such effort in refusing. 'The child is not our concern,' he said.

'A child is *everyone's* concern!' hissed Viv

Darch's blue eyes considered her coolly. 'Your ignorance suggests your mother kept you hidden. It would be wise to learn from the child as you journey.'

Viv glared at him but his attention was on the shield and it was only when he pulled it onto his lap she saw it was some sort of drum. It made the same melancholy music she had heard waking after Tarchen's attack, something her mother would have called *Rosie's Tunes* after Viv's Irish great, great grandmother.

Tarchen had the same instrument strapped to his pack and given he was ready to leave, Darch's little concert seemed strange. Darch ceased playing as suddenly as he began, secured the instrument to his pack, and heaved it on. Then he laid both palms on the ground and cocked his head as if he listened.

172

Viv glanced at Poss in mystification but the little girl was intent on poking the fire coals with a stick. Viv sensed a fine hum and for a horrible moment thought a rift was about to open and Thris leap out but the vibration came from *beneath* her feet.

Darch nodded in satisfaction and seemed about to follow Tarchen when he spoke. 'Go to Esh-accom,' he said. 'If the child's father lives, he'll be there.' Then he lowered his voice. 'Take care, *elddra*. He's a dangerous man, more dangerous than he knows.' His eyes held hers for a moment longer and then he was gone.

Darch's warning echoed in Viv's head as she surveyed their surroundings. The ruined buildings were even drearier in daylight and judging from the fragments in the rubble, had once been filled with beautiful things.

Poss still poked at the fire but it was not the play of a happy child but of one who could not bear to look about her. This was where she had grown up; laughed and chased with other children; been sung to sleep by her mother.

The Waradi bracelet lay in the dirt next to the fire and Viv picked it up and wiped it clean. 'The Scharii left it for you,' said Poss, her voice as dull as her eyes. 'Are you lein-trysted to a Waradi?'

'I'm not lein-trysted to anyone,' said Viv, guessing it was some sort of marriage arrangement. She turned the bracelet over in her hands, knowing she should toss it in the coals. It might be useful as trade, she countered, and pushed it back up under her sleeve. 'It was being used to make some birdmen fight,' she said, as she settled next to Poss. 'I took it to stop the fight.'

'They're called Lefer,' said Poss. 'The Valen don't go to the waste-woods but da says he'll take me to see the Lefer when I'm older. Serrid says they look like giant mouse-bats with red eyes, and claws like knives, and they screech all day.'

Viv picked up a stick and joined Poss in coal-poking. 'The Lefer I saw were a bit like bats but with lovely green feathers. They had claws on their wings that they used to climb, and they lived in nests that hung from the trees. One of them was kind to me when I was hurt.'

Poss nodded. 'Da says they have their own ways that are no better or worse than ours.'

There was a short silence and Viv dropped her stick into the coals. 'Darch said your da might be at Esh-accom,' she said. 'Do you know where that is?'

'I want to stay here.'

'There's nothing here anymore,' said Viv gently.

'There is, there is!' said Poss shrilly. 'Sita's here!'

'Sita?'

'My horse. I told her to stay away before Serrid took me to Esh-embrin. Da told her as well.' Poss's grubby hands had clenched as if she expected a fight.

'We'll see if we can find her, but we can't search for long. We have to get to Esh-accom.'

Poss nodded but instead of heading off into the trees she stood, cupped her hands around her mouth, and whistled. The sound was piercing and to Viv's alarm, she repeated it to each quarter of the clearing. Poss had just broadcast their presence to every murdering thug in the area but the horse did not appear and thankfully, neither did anything else.

'We have to go, Poss,' she said. 'We might come across Sita along the way. What does she look like?'

'Like an Eshadi horse of course,' snapped Poss. 'You don't know *anything*.'

'I told you I was a stranger in these parts,' said Viv, resisting the urge to snap back. 'You'll have to show me the way to Esh-accom.

'I don't know the way.'

Viv took a deep breath. 'Do you know the *direction* then?' Poss nodded and a tear tracked down her dirty cheek. 'Come,' said Viv gently and held her close until the storm of sobbing had passed. Poss's house was lost and possibly her da, and any help lay at a place neither of them knew how to get to. And just to add to the bloody joy, they had nothing to eat and no idea where the murdering thugs were.

'I don't suppose our musical friends left us any food?' she said. Poss shook her head. 'I didn't think so,' muttered Viv.

'We don't need their food when we've got our own,' said Poss.

Viv's spirits rose at the prospect of some sort of hidden cellar under the ruins but Poss set off towards the trees. There was a path there that led away up-hill with steps carved into its steeper parts and pockets of yellow flowers planted to either side. They were in full bloom and would hardly have escaped the thugs' attention but when they cleared the trees, there were no new ruins, just an emerald pool so beautiful Viv stopped in amazement. The water was greener than Glass Lake but the colour triggered memories of Thris's glorious face, crystal-beaded with water, as he had held her close.

'Viv! Come on!' Viv jerked her attention back to her surroundings. The pool was fed by a broad waterfall and its overflow cascaded away into a gully thick with yellow butterflies. Poss was already halfway across the ledge at the waterfall's base and as she disappeared behind the fall of water, Viv guessed there was a cave. It was hardly an original idea to use such places to hide things and as she hurried after Poss, she braced for more smashed walls and excrement.

There *was* a cave but Viv did not have the chance to discover if it were despoiled because Poss had disappeared. Viv's heart pounded as she stared at the empty ledge. Surely if Poss had fallen in Viv would have heard her? She hurried past the cave as fast as the ledge allowed and would have passed Poss had not a hand waved from the stone. There was a second cave, its narrow entrance made invisible by a deep overlap of mossy rock. It was a neat trick to use cave one as a decoy, conceded Viv, as she slid inside.

Cave two might have a narrow entrance but it was large and airy. Shelves driven into the stone were piled high with cloth-wrapped bundles, and there were rows of boxes and wooden kegs stacked around its sides. Herbs even hung drying from strings, as did something that looked like withered cactus.

'Blackbor,' said Poss disparagingly and brightened as she pointed to boxes of nuts and dried fruit, and helped herself to what looked like almonds.

It was a relief to find food they could take with them but they needed warm clothes too and Poss needed a shoe. Poss did not know what the cloth-wrapped bundles were but the material was stiff, as if treated with water-proofing and when Viv carefully unrolled one, she discovered women's clothes. There was something about the way they had been folded, with fragrant herbs strewn between the layers, that suggested their owner was dead.

'They were my mother's,' mumbled Poss, cheeks bulging with nuts. 'She chose da but she isn't with us anymore.'

Viv had no idea whether she had died or left, and did not ask, having had to fend off questions about her own mother as a child. She did not want to take clothes special to Poss and her da, especially as she had no hope of ever returning them, but she needed a shirt and jacket, and Poss needed a jacket *and* shoe.

Viv repacked the bundle and opened another but it contained men's clothing that was too big. A third bundle contained children's clothes that were too small, even for Poss. 'I'm beginning to feel like Goldilocks,' muttered Viv, as she unwrapped a fourth bundle that contained children's clothes again. 'Was this yours when you were younger?' she asked, holding up a dress.

Poss shrugged. 'It might have been Tarly's or one of the other girl's.'

'Tarly?'

'*Tarlieh*. Serrid's daughter.'

Viv took a steadying breath as more puzzle pieces fell into place. Poss's da had obviously expected trouble and sent Poss's horse away and had Serrid, no doubt someone he trusted, take Poss to Esh-embrin, which Viv guessed was the burned settlement where she had exited the rift. Given that Poss was alone, Serrid and the other little girl probably lay among the burned and mutilated corpses.

'This should be kaest nuts but it's things from the house,' said Poss, clearly puzzled. She had opened a keg and its contents gleamed even in the cave's dim light. Viv lifted out a silver candlestick, beautifully tooled and set with smooth blue and green gems. 'That sits on the

177

table in the eating-hall,' said Poss, 'and this is mine,' she added, holding up a hand mirror.

It was silver too and as Poss looked at herself in it, Viv saw its back was engraved with a robed figure adorned with artistically elongated wings. 'What's that?' she asked hoarsely.

Poss flicked the mirror over. 'Oh, that's an Astraali,' she said, 'from Astraal.'

Chapter 33

For someone who was completely distracted, Viv organised the clothing and portioned the food with ruthless efficiency. The screws at the Juvenile Detention Facility would have been proud, she concluded dourly. She modified her own shirt to make a jacket for Poss and sacrificed the back of one of the children's thick jackets to make a shoe, and used its sleeves to make pouches to carry nuts and blackbor. Then she gave one to Poss to carry in case they were separated.

Viv took the clothes that belonged to Poss's mother because it was either that or freeze and freezing was not going to help Poss. The clothes were intricately patterned and Viv hoped they would help her fit in. Regardless, they were clean and warm and her spirits rose.

Poss was happier too and uncharacteristically chatty. Viv learned that as well as having the finest horses in Eshavale, Poss's da had the finest urrut, and whatever could not be produced in their val, he procured from the *Stonash* or from Esh-accom during the *festivities*. Given Poss's description, Viv guessed that urrut were a fleece animal and the Stonash were traders whose wares included finer things such as *amé casques*.

Viv had learned of *amé casques* when she had removed her shirt to alter it for Poss. The little girl had been anxious about how Viv had lost her casque and after a while Viv understood Poss referred to the cloth bundle at her neck. The ragged cloth contained Thris's feather that Viv had saved when she believed him dead, and it remained precious despite knowing he lived.

Poss had then revealed an exquisite gold filigreed cylinder she wore concealed beneath her clothes. 'You must have a better casque to honour and protect your amé,' she told Viv solemnly. 'Da will trade a beautiful one for you.'

Viv guessed an amé was some sort of religious object, like a cross, but she had more pressing problems than amé casques. She could find no water bottle and that meant they must stay within a day's march of water *if* that were possible and still reach Esh-accom.

The good news was that Poss *did* know where Esh-accom was after all, because she suddenly parroted a description that probably came from her da. *Climb three ridges sunwise, then journey straight starwise.* It took careful questioning for Viv to discover sunwise was east and starwise south. Having to climb four more ridges was daunting but at least turning south meant the final leg of the journey *should* be down a valley which *should* be easier, or so she hoped.

They set off but Poss was teary again at abandoning Sita and Viv told her story about another horse to distract her. She chose one about Thowra, a silver brumby hunted because of his unusual colour. Viv had been about Poss's age when she had discovered the silver brumby stories and had loved them, probably because Thowra always out ran those who meant him harm.

Poss seemed to enjoy the story too and after a while told Viv more about Sita without getting upset. Viv learned that Poss was given Sita as a foal and that Sita had been bred from da's horses. Unsurprisingly, da's horses were not only the finest in Eshavale but Eshadi horses the finest of *all* the Vales.

'Because they're born in Eshavale?' teased Viv.

'Because they *know* us and are the most beautiful. They have dark grey coats and silver manes and tails, like Thowra,' added Poss. 'Da says when you're high in the Vale and a storm whips foam from the Argine, it's like Eshadi horses are racing across the sky.'

Viv's stomach clenched as she recalled the odd coloured horses at the cock-fight. 'What colour are the other Vales' horses?' she asked carefully.

'Ascavale horses are dark grey with black manes and tails, Warinavale black with brown manes and tails, Genessavale chestnut all over, I think . . .' Poss trailed off. 'I can't remember the rest but Da says they're all different. The other Vales are further away.'

The cock-fighters had probably been Waradi then, concluded Viv, which fitted with the Waradi tryst-bracelet. She had no idea which Vale the *bad men* came from but it would be safest to steer clear of anyone riding horses *not* dark grey with a silver manes and tails.

The weather stayed fine but Viv did not know whether the season was the equivalent of summer or they were just lucky. They might be in for rain, sleet, snow, or some weird meteorological event for all she knew and yet the lands were so like home Viv might have enjoyed the trek had she not found herself peering over her shoulder.

They kept to the trees but the trees eventually gave way to low bushes and then to grasses that forced them to walk in the open. Viv wished to God she knew which way the murdering bastards headed. There was dung amongst the grass but Viv saw no animals including the mysterious *urrut*. There were birds though and she watched them as they walked.

When Thris had told her about folds, she expected them to be full of bizarre plants and animals, but the ones she had visited were not that different to Australia. It made sense, she supposed, that similar life-forms such as birds inhabited them too but the use of English made no sense at all.

The Keeper in Hearth Fold spoke English, as did Poss, and Tarchen and Darch although they spoke another language too. Even Ezam's angels spoke English. Perhaps it *was* the language of the gods after all, as her old English teacher had joked.

Small birds flicked in the grasses and bigger ones soared overhead and Viv smiled as she imagined teasing Thris about them. 'Are you thinking about your *friend* Thrisdane?' asked Poss, her shrewd eyes on Viv's face.

'Yes,' said Viv taken aback.

'Are you lein-trysted to him?'

'No,' said Viv but her face warmed and Poss smirked, reminding Viv of the girls at school who whispered about boys behind the shelter shed.

'When we're older, Tarly and I are going to choose our lein-trysts from among the Sylds,' boasted Poss. 'They're the strongest and most handsome of the Valen, like da. You could choose a lein-tryst now, Viv. You're so pretty you could have anyone.'

Darch had mentioned *sylds* but Viv had no idea what they were except she suspected an Astraali bastard was not high on their wish list, not that she cared. She had no intention of giving any man the legal right to beat the crap out of her. 'I think we should look for somewhere to rest and eat,' she said. 'Is there water nearby?'

'All vals have rills,' said Poss in the resigned tone she used when stating the obvious.

'The val between Eralia and Serier Ridges didn't,' retorted Viv, sick of feeling stupid.

'That's not a val,' said Poss dismissively. 'Vals run cloudwise-starwise.'

Viv added this latest crumb of information to the pile. Vals ran north-south *and* had *rills* that Viv assumed were streams. The valleys that ran east and west, or sunwise-starwise, were *not* called vals and did *not* have streams, in fact, the one between Eralia and Serier had no water at all. And all these little valleys or *vals* were in one *big* Vale called Eshavale.

Poss had named seven other Vales and Viv presumed they contained little valleys running north-south as well. If they were like Eshavale and fanned out from the cloud-wreathed peak with its central city of Astraal, it was pretty bloody obvious why Darch had called the fold *The Wheel*.

The rill, that Poss said was called *Seman*, turned out to be a narrow, fast flowing stream, and cold enough to be meltwater which made sense given the snowy peak Viv had glimpsed when pursued by the red-crested birdman. She copied Poss's thanking ceremony and drank, enjoying the chill slide of water down her throat. It was useful to have no need to regularly eat or drink but Viv longed to harmonise. Thris had been right that she needed to align to feel truly well but she was reluctant to do so front of Poss and it was too risky to leave her.

It was cool near the stream and not just because the ridge shaded the valley floor. Cloud had rolled in and a

183

wind sprung up that soon whined through the val in a high-pitched wail. Poss called it an *asht*-voice but Viv was more concerned about how to cross the Seman than any *asht-voices*.

It was raining before they found a scatter of stones to get to the other side and while the next slope was steeper, at least it had trees to shelter under. They stopped to don warmer clothes but Poss was reluctant to wear Viv's shirt. 'It's got no patterning,' she complained, as Viv secured it with a ragged belt.

'I told you I'm not from the Vales, Poss.'

'Then you must be Astraali.'

Poss's face had taken on its suspicious, fearful look and Viv crouched in front of her. 'When I was very young, I used to play in my room and then as I grew, I played in the trees out the back. Because I was little, they were the only places I knew. They were my whole world. Was it like that for you too, Poss? Did you only start to explore more places when you were bigger?' Poss nodded gravely. 'As I grew older, I went further and further and saw more and more things,' continued Viv. 'All these new things were like other worlds.'

'Da took me to Esh-seman last Horse Zadic,' volunteered Poss. 'I had honeyed shallit.'

'And there are places beyond Esh-seman?' asked Viv. Poss nodded. 'And places beyond those?' Again the nod. 'So, you see there are many different worlds beyond your house and the waterfall and pool, and Esh-seman,' said Viv.

'Yes, but they're all in The Wheel,' said Poss, 'and the people all have patterns.' Viv could think of no counter argument and felt Poss's small hand clutch hers. 'I don't mind if you're *elddra*, Viv,' she said softly. 'Da won't

184

mind either. The Scharii make lovely music and da always welcomes them but he says ...' she paused her brows kinked in concentration. 'He says they *know* a lot but they *feel* nothing.'

The trees provided shelter from the rain but their clashing branches made it hard to hear anything like the approach of others and Poss's revelations about the elddra added to Viv's tension. If the Astraali were angels, as the engraved mirror suggested, then Darch and Poss were right, she was elddra, presuming elddra meant a half-angel.

A child like Poss might accept her but given Tarchen's reaction, Poss's da certainly would not; the Astraali so despised their bastards were hidden away. Hiding *bastard off-spring* also strengthened the case for the Astraali being angels because Valen women would not sleep with the detested Astraali *unless* their beauty overwhelmed their prejudices.

Viv wondered whether the Valen's antagonism was jealousy or whether the Astraali had some murderous trait no one had bothered to be mention. Darch suggested Tarchen's hostility stemmed from some sort of personal injury so it was possible.

The rain grew and Viv headed deeper into the trees where the canopy was thicker, but the undergrowth was thicker too and tangled with briars. 'Fine if you're Br'er Rabbit,' muttered Viv, as she struggled through. Thunder boomed and as rain pelted, she found a tunnel under the briars and dragged Poss in behind her.

The enclosed space provided good shelter but held a stink Viv had smelled before. 'Maragh,' whispered Poss, dark eyes wide.

'What . . .' began Viv then heard a grunt that froze her blood. God in heaven! A pig-bear!

Chapter 34

Ataghan en-Scinta-ril brought his horse to a stop in a
brilliant shaft of star-sheen. It was one of the few to
penetrate the trees and illuminated his raised hand and the
flick of his fingers. Those he led slid silently from their
mounts. Their clothing blended with the forest's shadows
as did their horses, their silver manes and tails dyed black.

The Pool Zadic's brightness filled the night sky but
the marl- and raffinwoods gave the men the cover they
needed. Ataghan dismounted, cupped Taris's muzzle
between his hands and breathed slow instructions. His
men followed suit. Like Ataghan, they gave their horses
permission to take another rider should their present one
not return. Then the horses obediently moved off into the
darkness.

A man came to Ataghan's side and they crept forward
to the edge of a camp where dark shapes slept around a
smouldering fire. The sleepers had set no guards for they
slept in their own Vale.

'Seventeen,' the man whispered to Ataghan. 'They
might have women with them,' he added and swore
softly. 'That complicates things.'

'Their choice, Sehereden.'

'We can't—'

Ataghan's hand chopped down and there was a tense
silence, then he mimicked the hunting call of a geist-
owl and his men moved into position. A second call sent
them swarming forward, knives flashing. Ataghan led,
stabbing and slashing with such precision half of those he
despatched barely woke before he sent them into death.

A woman scrambled away, her scream cut short as his knife found her back, and by the time he had retrieved it, the only sound was his men's harsh breathing. Two had suffered slash wounds and Ataghan summoned the band's surgeon before he went to where the Ascadi horses were tethered. Their eyes were white-ringed with fear and he sang to them softly until they calmed, then glanced back to where his men built a pyre. 'Brithergen,' he called, and one of his men hurried over.

'Syld?'

'Drive a nail into the front hoof of every horse then turn them loose.'

'A nail, Syld?'

Ataghan's eyes flashed. 'Unless you prefer to send them the same way as their riders? I'm not delivering transport to another mob of Ascadi murderers.' Brithergen nodded and Ataghan strode back to where Sehereden oversaw the stacking of bodies. 'They'll be no pyre, Sehereden. We'll give them to the Ascacade.'

The firelight revealed Sehereden's shock. 'Valen-lore dictates we send them back to the stars.'

'Valen-lore dictates Valen remain crest-bound, that no woman *or* child be harmed! Let them be grateful I let them take their amés into death.'

Sehereden clipped out an order and the men dragged the bodies to the cade's edge and rolled them into the water. Ataghan's band was high in the Vale and the Ascacade's flow fast here, and the men watched the corpses bob and swirl away. Some would be taken by maragh, others by gytars, but some would reach the higher setts.

They would be bloated, their soft parts eaten out by slipfins, but Ataghan hoped they would still be recognisable. He wanted those who had known them in life to know the Eshadi's anger.

The pyre roared as his men burned the horses' harness and Ataghan's lip curled. The Ascadi must bind their horses to their wills with leather and metal unlike the Eshadi horses who carried their riders willingly.

His band had discharged his orders with brutal efficiency and he expected no less. Three zadics had passed since the Waradi had breached the crests but less than one since the Ascadi had followed. They had waited like maragh in their burrows for the stench of rotting flesh to tempt them out, and it had come soon enough, Eshadi murdered as they slept. The old, the women and—

Ataghan rammed his knife-blade into his palm and fought to control his breathing as Sehereden came to his side. 'We await your orders, Syld,' he said.

Syld, not Ataghan, or *lein*, as Sehereden was entitled to call him. Sehereden was angry Ataghan had violated Valen-lore but Sehereden did not understand Valen-lore had ended the night Waradi blades had found those of Esh-embrin.

Sehereden's gaze flicked to Ataghan's bloodied hand. 'Lein . . .'

'We need supplies,' clipped out Ataghan, his gaze on his men. 'We'll go starwise and find an Ascadi sett. Given the cade's filth will have reached them first, it should be deserted. If not . . .' he shrugged. 'We'll load up and re-cross. I need to be in Esh-accom to meet the other Sylds, not that I expect the meeting to be useful.'

Sehereden seemed about to speak but Ataghan whistled and Taris emerged from the darkness. Ataghan's whistle used notes familiar to all Eshadi horses and

189

notes special to Taris and as other whistles sounded, the remainder of the horses appeared. Taris rubbed his face against Ataghan's jacket and Ataghan caressed him with his sound hand then vaulted on and when his band had mounted, gave Taris permission to go.

Ataghan's senses were tuned to the forest as well as to those who followed. Pool Zadic flung the band's shadows stark across the ground where the trees thinned but Ataghan kept to the densest stands. They were deep in Ascavale with a perilous crest climb between them and Eshavale's safety. There was *no* safety. His blood burned and he flexed his hand to reopen the wound.

Even had Ataghan been blind-folded, he would have known he was in an alien Vale. The scent of the raffinwoods was less intense, the cry of the geist-owls higher pitched, the chitter of mouse-bats quicker. Daylight would reveal other differences too: the leaf-lilters' breasts more yellow than green, the sendrass's blooms more purple than blue.

Only soaring crests divided the Vales, not easy to scale on horseback but not impossible *if* you knew the way, *if* you had reason to risk your neck and that of your horse, *if* your hatred were strong enough. It had not been the crests that had kept the peace for so long, it had been Valen-lore but Valen-lore lay cold and dead in Esh-embrin's ashes, along with everything else he loved.

They stopped when Pool Zadic gave way to the softer blush of stars but Ataghan remained mounted, his gaze on the dying constellation. He half hoped for the brief, secondary blaze of the Call Zadic that all Valen hoped for, but it did not come.

Had he been alone, he would have ridden all night, but his men could not if they must fight off attack, not that attack was likely so high in the Vale. The Ascadi favoured the gentler vals starwise but Ataghan still searched the air. Taris was at ease and after a while his tension eased too. Valen horses sensed each other regardless of the Vale of their foaling but only Eshavale horses passed their thoughts to their riders.

By the time Ataghan dismounted, Sehereden had organised the camp and guards. He had adapted to the fighting quickly, but it was no less than Ataghan expected. Since they had stumbled across each other *and* the maragh all those zadicans ago, then sworn leinship covered in its blood and their own, Sehereden had never given Ataghan cause for doubt.

Being lein meant sharing everything but there were things buried so deep in Ataghan that not even Sehereden's love could reach and there were things Ataghan chose *not* to share like his first breach of the crests.

He could not recall when the frisson in his blood had first started but he had learned not to ignore it and had gone where only Scharii trod, crossing sunwise into Warinavale first, and then nightwise into Ascavale. Neither Vale showed signs of want or war and he had learned nothing useful *except* that he could breach the crests undetected thanks to his *magical* powers.

He smiled sourly. The *mighty* Ataghan who felt no fear, who *smelled* danger, whose Astraal-touched knives never went astray. One out of three was not bad, he conceded. The sureness of his blades had nothing to do with the cloud-crawlers in their city of ice, and fear lived

in him like a maggot in a corpse, but he *could* smell
when things were rotten and the air was putrid.

Taris moved restlessly as he picked up Ataghan's
disquiet, and Ataghan gave the big stallion permission
to follow the other horses down to the water's edge. He
watched him go, hating the dye in Taris's mane and tail.
It parodied the lesser Ascadi horses, which was the point,
he reminded himself.

He turned away from the murmured conversations of
his men and strode off through the trees.

Milk-moths rose in pale clouds and a geist-owl
glided through the canopy as his quick passage disturbed
its roost. He searched for a koachar and stopped when
he found one big enough for his purpose. Koachars set
their branches high and Ataghan ran at it and used a
well-placed boot to launch himself skyward. Even so,
he almost missed the branch and re-opened the cut to his
hand.

The next branch was well above him and he grimaced.
It seemed he must earn his view of the val. The Lefer
used wing-claws to climb but he had his knives. He
bound his wounded hand to stop it slipping and used
the same technique as the Lefer as he plunged each of
his knives into the bark in turn, and swung himself up.
His breath exploded in grunts but he reached the next
branch and rested. Not one of his more graceful efforts,
he conceded.

The branch above was reachable with a single spring
but the one after that trickier. Koachars were not easy
climbs and this one had enjoyed hundreds of zadicans
to make itself contrary. Ataghan toiled on, glad of his
excellent balance, but taking nothing for granted.

The canopy dropped away but he did not stop until the

koachar's trunk tapered, then he propped himself against it and stared out over the val. He saw the glint of the Ascacade, bright as a ribbon of Astraal silver, and heard its fall from the Argine behind him but he did not look that way. He stared starwise, towards the enemy.

No one remembered why Valen-lore had dictated Valen keep to their own Vales. Each Vale might have provided for its inhabitants without the need to risk the precipitous crests, or there might have been fighting before. Whatever the case, only Scharii had regularly traversed the crests *until now*.

He saw nothing untoward, and as heat surged, he leapt down to the next branch, swung hand over hand around the bole, and leapt again. He plunged down the tree without pause, one slip away from death, and landed with a bone-jarring thud on the forest floor. *Mad At*, he thought bitterly, as he strode back to camp. His men had named him well.

Chapter 35

Viv froze; for a horrible moment she thought the pig-bear was in the tunnel with them, but the grunt came from behind and she screwed her head around. It was some distance away, nosing in the leaf litter but headed their way. Viv's thoughts raced. She knew pig-bears were fast with tusks like razors *and* that they were easily distracted *and* that they could not climb trees.

'It's seen us,' whispered Poss.

Or smelled us, thought Viv. It stared straight at them, unblinking despite the rain, then lowered its head. Viv had the wild idea of flying them both to safety but Poss had bolted last time Viv had frightened her. 'See that tree?' she hissed. 'As soon as that thing is chasing me, climb it as fast as you can. Don't stop and don't look back.'

'You can't . . .' gasped Poss.

'Do it!' ordered Viv and scrambled from the tunnel. The pig-bear swung in her direction and she ran for her life. Her only hope lay in speed but this was not the smooth floor of the Dendrinai and it was slick with rain. She slipped, windmilled her arms, regained her balance, and hurtled on leaping logs and bushes. Then the ground suddenly disappeared in front of her and she pitched headlong into a gully. Viv gave a strangled shriek and threw up her hands.

Nothing happened. The pig-bear had stopped on the rim, distracted by something to its right.

God in Heaven! It was Ky! He was on the ground, wings flapping erratically, his face filled with confusion, and then he saw the pig-bear and screamed. The pig-bear charged and there was a burst of light as Thris flashed into existence, snatched up Ky, and was swallowed by the air.

Viv scrambled up and with an explosive burst of speed, reached the nearest tree and swung herself into its branches. The tree shook as the pig-bear rammed it, squealing in fury, and Viv heard Poss's screams above the ruckus.

'I'm safe,' she yelled back, terrified Poss would come looking for her. 'I'm safe Poss, stay where you are! Stay where you are!' Poss's screams dissolved into sobs and Viv continued to shout reassuringly but her whole being trilled with the wonder of Thris. His exquisite purple eyes had not turned in her direction but he *must* have sensed her presence and would come back for her.

The rain continued and Viv remained crouched in the tree, cold and wet, long after the pig-bear had wandered off. It was close to dark before she dared swing herself down and creep back to Poss's tree. The little girl was too frightened to descend and Viv had to climb up and carry her down. 'You really are a possum now,' she said lightly, as she reached the ground.

'You went into a *maragh* tunnel,' accused Poss.

Viv said nothing, simply set off upslope with Poss still clinging to her. The rain dwindled and as the cloud drifted away and more star-sheen reached the ground, she quickened her pace and reached the ridge-top by Pool Zadic's light and set Poss down. Only one more ridge to go before they turned south, or starwise, as Poss would have it, and then the journey should be easier, she consoled herself.

Poss sat huddled on a stone and Viv glanced at her worriedly. She needed to be out of her wet clothes and into a warm bed. *Not a problem, Vivi. There's a lovely hotel just around the corner. They even have hot cocoa.* A cave will do, Rim, Viv retorted silently, or better still, a box of matches. 'What do they use to light fires around here?' she muttered, half to herself.

'Oilstone,' said Poss dully. 'There's some in the store cave at home.'

It would have been handy to know that *before* they set out, thought Viv sourly, but she was more annoyed with herself than Poss. She had been so busy congratulating herself on getting her hands on food and clothing, and so keen to find a water bottle, she had forgotten a pretty bloody obvious thing like fire.

Pool Zadic made the night as bright as day and Viv decided it was pointless lingering on the ridge top with no shelter and no fire. 'We'll keep going,' she said, 'and if it's fine tomorrow, we'll rest and dry our clothes.'

'I don't feel well,' said Poss.

Viv laid her hand across Poss's forehead but had no idea whether the little girl was too warm. She was subdued though and Viv bit her lip. She had read that before penicillin was invented, people died from all sorts of small things even the common cold.

'How about I carry you again?' she said and forced a grin as if it were all part of some happy little game. Poss nodded and Viv hoisted her onto her back and tried not to think of what would happen if Poss really were ill. Lots of places used herbs to cure things but Viv had no idea what medicinal herbs grew at home, let alone here and if Poss *were* ill, Viv's best bet would be to high-tail it to Esh-accom without delay.

They should be there in a day or two anyway, depending on how far south or *starwise* it was. It might

196

even be sooner if they came across some mounted Eshadi and hitched a ride, or better still, the Eshadi took Poss to her da. Then Viv could go on her way. The prospect of being free of Poss did not bring the relief she expected. Poss was just a detour on the way to her mother, she reminded herself, but she was going to miss the little girl.

Her spirits rose as the darkness faded. Her worst experiences on the streets had been at night when refuges became traps and new friends predators. It was as if the darkness ate all hope. Poss's cheek was hot against Viv's neck but Viv could go no faster, the slope slippery with the night's rain, and it was close to midday before she reached the stream at the bottom, eased Poss down, and rubbed her aching back.

'What is *this* rill called?' she asked but Poss sat with her head hanging. Viv tried again. 'You should have a drink.'

'I want to sleep.'

'Drink and then we'll find a nice sunny spot to snuggle down in,' cajoled Viv.

Poss drank but she was unsteady and Viv knew she would have to be carried again. This time Viv made a sling out of her jacket by knotting the sleeves around her neck, hefting Poss into it, and tying the tails behind her. It was easier on her back and left her hands free but while Poss was soon asleep, Viv had never been more awake, horribly aware she had now added caring for a sick child to dodging murderous mobs and vicious pig-bears.

And then, right on cue, she smelled smoke. Shit! So far smoke had meant burned settlements and corpses, tortured birdmen, and the stinking Scharii, and even if it heralded none of these things, whoever owned it was unlikely to befriend an Astraali bastard.

It could belong to an Eshadi, she countered, but
not the way her luck was running. She crept on until
she came to a rocky cliff face. The smoke drifted from
a cave a little way up but it was so quiet that birds
fluttered about the entranceway. Maybe the camp had
been abandoned and the fire left to burn itself out. *Yeah,
sure Vivi. There's a table up there too, set with linen and
silverware and reserved in ya name.*

Viv edged back into the trees. Poss's face was flushed
and her hair lay in damp tendrils. She needed warmth
and she needed fluids *now* and Viv could offer neither.
She back-tracked, found a tree with dense foliage and
climbed. When the ground was hidden from view, she
fastened the sling with Poss in it to a sturdy branch and
hooked the food packs nearby. Poss's feet dangled out the
end and Viv's last glimpse of her, as she climbed down,
was of the makeshift shoe.

The cave might or might not be deserted but Viv circled
wide to the slope above, wriggled forward, and peered
into it. Her vantage point gave her a good view of the
smouldering fire but nothing else and cursing under her
breath, she picked her way down through the bushes to the
side and crouched behind a tumble of stone.

The cave disappeared into darkness but a pack and
neatly rolled blanket sat a little way in and adrenaline
surged. Its owner must be near but the pack would have
a water bottle or mug but she needed both to carry water
and to scoop up some coals. *Get in quick, get out quicker.*
The thieves' mantra rang in her head and she darted to
the pack. It was laced and, made clumsy by fear, seemed
to take forever for her to open. She thrust her hand in and

her fingers passed over odd bundles then the shape of a water bottle and a mug's cool metal.

'You can die now or put your hands on your head and live a little longer.' A man's silhouette blocked the cave's entrance, blades in both hands. 'Hands on your head,' he ordered, 'unless you're chosen option one.' Viv's shaking hands went her head. 'Out! Now!'

She forced herself forward and when she neared him, he seized her arm and kicked her legs from under her. His knee ground into her back as rope bit around her wrists then he wrenched her upright. For a moment he simply stared and then he laughed ironically. 'Well, well, well. We meet again.'

It was the Waradi man from the Leferen who had chased her on a horse then lost her to the pig-bear attack. He laughed again, this time with real humour. 'And today,' he said softly, 'I'm not expecting any interruptions to our little meeting.'

Ataghan gripped the top of Esh-accom's wall and leaned forward into the darkness. Wind whipped the hair from his face but he knew it spent its fury high in Dart-val and that the asht-voices would be thunderous there. Light spilled from the crowded buildings behind him but he did not turn and then a child's laughter sounded and his blood burned.

He reached for his knife but he was no longer alone. 'Not a good night to be outside the halls, lein,' said Sehereden, his gaze also beyond the wall. Ataghan made no reply and Sehereden lounged against the parapet as if he sought only the night's fresher air. 'Darthen agrees with Mathian,' he said softly. 'Do nothing and our enemies fade away.'

'And Garath?' asked Ataghan, his gaze on the plains.

'Believes we've bought the fighting on ourselves by breaching the crests. Kurnen isn't in yet but he's likely to side with Garath.'

Ataghan's knuckles whitened as he considered the other Sylds. Waradi *and* Ascadi attacks had started well before any retaliation and the other Sylds had yet to lose more than urrut but they would, maybe even this night as they relaxed at their hearths. And he was no better, idling his time away here while Waradi and Ascadi murdered at will.

The wind grew and the keen of asht-voices added to the sear of his blood. 'I'm going back,' he said abruptly.

Sehereden gripped his arm. 'You've only just come in. Even *you* need to rest sometimes, lein.'

'Not Mad At,' said Ataghan bitterly.

'Even you, my brother.'

Sehereden's touch eased the burn of Ataghan's blood as it always did but then they heard shouts and the pound of horses on the plain. Ataghan took the wall steps two at a time, Sehereden at his heels and then the gate creaked open and the yard filled with horses, cries and the stench of blood and sweat. Some horses carried two while others were riderless. There were women clutching babies and children and men with their possessions strapped to their backs.

The melee parted to admit Ataghan and Sehereden, and Kurnen slipped from his horse and would have hit the cobblestones had Ataghan not caught him. Sehereden issued quick commands and the chaos gave way to the billeting of the arrivals and the stabling of horses, while Ataghan took the flask someone handed him and half poured the contents down Kurnen's throat.

The young Syld coughed violently but his colour returned and he could speak. A Waradi attack, Esh-min razed, the survivors a third of those who had dwelt there. If Kurnen had not been passing with a band bound for Esh-accom, there would have been none left to tell the tale *like Esh-embrin*. As it was, the young Syld had still lost four of his men and suffered a savage knife wound to his thigh.

Sehereden returned to Ataghan's side as Kurnen was helped away. 'We're going after them?' he asked.

Ataghan nodded, already striding towards the stables. 'I want Anthran, Sandagh, Inaghan, Enashen and Daran,' he clipped out. 'And capes,' he added, as the rain began.

'Not a full band?' asked Sehereden in surprise. 'The rest of the men will—'

'I need the agilest horses, Sehereden. We'll ride Soaich's Spine and cut the Waradi filth off *if* you're willing.'

'I'll follow wherever you lead, Syld, as your men will.'

'Then let's hope it's not into death,' said Ataghan, and disappeared into the darkness.

End of Angel Caste: Book 2 Angel Breath

You can continue Viv's story in Book 3 Angel Bone

Amazon US - https://www.amazon.com/dp/ B071VBNTSM
Amazon Australia - https://www.amazon.com.au/dp/ B071VBNTSM
Amazon Canada - https://www.amazon.ca/dp/ B071VBNTSM

Take a peek at Book 3

It was quiet, the only sound the rush of the rill, and
Viv struggled to calm. These could be her last moments
of life and she looked away from the men and corpses,
and up to the sky. It was silvered with dusk, but dawn
was her favourite time, the moment when the light
chased away the dark. She tightened her grip on the
feather at her neck. In an odd way, Thris would be with
her here, at the end and then, inexplicably, she heard
bells. The men who loitered near the corpses heard them
too and turned.

'Light the pyre!' the first man ordered, and his men
leapt into action, smashing rocks under booted-heels and
tossing them on. The driftwood they had packed around
the bodies caught first, followed by the clothing, and then
the smoke blackened as the flames found fat.

The man hauled Viv to her feet, but his gaze was on
Sehereden. 'It seems our problems are solved, lein,' he
said, and dragged her towards the fire.

Every picture Viv had ever seen of witch-burnings
smashed back into her head and she kicked and clawed
at him with all her strength. Sehereden followed, his
expression impassive.

'Our Waradi lein-tryst doesn't like the heat,' the man
grunted, as he wrestled her forward. 'Which is just as
well, given she's to return to her maker.'

'You're sending her with the Stonash?'

'*You* won't have her killed, lein, and *I* won't have her left. She'll travel the crests, back to the cloud-crawlers who seeded her.'

'She won't survive the journey.'

'Why not, lein? Every Valen knows the elddra do not suffer as we do.' He twisted Viv's arm up her back and, as she shrieked and doubled over in pain, wrenched the feather from her neck, and dangled it before her eyes.

'You'll go into death without your amé to guide you,' he said harshly. 'See it as a reward for those you've sent on ahead of you.' And with that, he threw the feather into the fire.

Viv's scream was so primal those who watched clutched their own amés. She was aware of being dragged away from the fire's heat, but of little else. Pain consumed her, not just the physical pain of her injuries, but something more profound, as if the very core of her had been wounded.

I hope you enjoyed *Angel Caste* Book 2 – *Angel Breath*.
Authors need reviews! It is how our readers find us.
I would love you to leave me an honest review on
Amazon, Goodreads, or another of your favourite reader
sites. Read on to discover my other books.

Works by K S Nikakis
Available on Amazon KDP and a range of digital
platforms.

Non Fiction

**Journey: Seeking the Sacred, Spirit and Soul in the
Australian Wilderness**

Deadway - Finalist Best Poem
2020 Australian Shadows Awards

When we set out into the wilderness, what is it we *really*
seek?

Do we seek new sights or do we seek new selves? And
are we *really* on one journey or on two?

Journeying fifteen thousand kilometres into Australia's
blood-red heart, Nikakis discovers that every journey is
perilous, for travellers risk carrying the clutter of their
outer lives with them; a clutter that blinds them to the
other journey they crave; that of the inner *soul-journey*
into a deeper understanding of self.

To enter Australia's vast Outback wilderness, is to enter
a place of endless horizons; a place doused with brilliant

gold dawns and dazzling sunsets; a place silvered by star-encrusted night skies and, most importantly, a place of hidden sacred places in whose deep stillness our inner journeys can at last unfold.

In the spirit of travellers like Robert Macfarlane and Scott Stillman, Nikakis asks what it is we really see, feel and understand when we follow in the steps of those who have gone before us deep into the wilderness.

Drawing on her Ph.D. in Joseph Campbell's hero myth, and using original poetry and novel extracts, Nikakis takes us on this second journey; a journey of the sacred, spirit and soul, where our inner selves finally have the time and space to gift us richer and more fully-realised lives.

Fantasy Novel Series

Angel Caste 5 Book Series – available complete in one book or as five individual books: Angel Blood, Angel Breath, Angel Bone, Angel Bound, Angel Blessed.

Angel Caste – Complete 5 Book Series - *A modern female hero on a timeless quest*

A troubled street kid, an angel guide, a binding promise . . .

Viv is on day release from jail to attend the funeral of the thug she thinks is her father, when her real father turns up, the powerful angel Archae Kald. If that is not shocking enough, Viv discovers her mother is not dead after all but lost somewhere in the tangle of worlds called the Rynth.

Determined to find the only person who ever loved her, Viv rift transits to Kald's angel world where he assigns the beautiful Thris to guide her to her mother. Thris is different to every male Viv has ever known but after a life on the streets, she finds it impossible to trust.

Thris trains her to travel the rifts, but the Rynth is a dark and dangerous place, even for angels and when Viv's angel traits emerge, disaster strikes. Lost and alone in the Rynth, Viv stumbles on a lost child in a war zone, and pledges to take the child to safety. But in the perilous worlds of the Rynth, deciding who is friend and who is foe is a deadly game of chance.

Bound by his pledge to guide Viv to her mother, Thris embarks on a desperate search for her, but a greater threat confronts them both and they must fight not just for their own lives, but for the lives of those they love.

The Kira Chronicles - 6 Book Series – available complete in one book or as six individual books: The Whisper of Leaves, The Silence of Stone, The Secrets of Stars, The Thunder of Hoofs, The Crying of Birds, The Music of Home.

The Kira Chronicles – Complete 6 Book Series –
traditional fantasy with deep forests and high stakes

A gold-eyed Healer, a prophecy, two brothers at war.

In seasons long past, twin gold-eyed princes sundered a kingdom. Rejecting his brother Terak's warrior ways, Kasheron led his people deep into the great southern forests and established the healing settlement of Allogrenia. The Tremen flourished, upholding Kasheron's legacy of peace and healing, and protected by the vast, trackless trees.

All Tremen delight in the healing arts, but Kira is the greatest Healer of them all.

To the north of Allogrenia, drought ravages the Shargh's land, and as their suffering escalates, the chief's younger brother seizes on an ancient prophecy to snatch the chiefship for himself. The prophecy links the Shargh's doom to a gold-eyed Healer, and Kira has gold eyes.

The Shargh attack with devastating consequences and Kira must fight to save the wounded, but the Shargh wounds rot, no matter her skill, and Kira finds herself in a deadly race against time. As the slaughter continues, she makes the horrifying discovery that the Shargh hunt *her*. To halt the attacks and save her people, she sets off for the North to seek aid from her long sundered warrior kin.

But the dangers beyond the forests exceed even the Shargh attacks. The Tremen detest their warrior kin but Terak's descendants have inflicted a worse fate on the Tremen. Kira's new-found love is torn apart by ancient hostilities and when trust turns to betrayal, it risks everything she fought for.

As the battles rage on, Kira becomes increasingly sickened by the bloodshed. Desperate to end the suffering once and for all, she sets out on a quest that could cost her everything and everyone she loves.

Fantasy Novels

The Emerald Serpent – *the Celtic Fae in a fight for survival*

Book trailer: https://www.youtube.com/watch?v=bGpKxnpCEMg

Betrayal, torture, death: Etaine lives on only to destroy those who robbed her of everything she loved.

Seven years before, Etaine met fellow Ranger Cormac, the Eadar she believed was her longed-for true-mate. Emerald-eyed, white-skinned, and black-haired, the Eadar had formed into Ranger bands to fight the Fada, invading religious zealots determined to replace the Eadar's Serpent Goddess with their own gods of stone.

The pure blood of the ancient Eadar runs strong in Etaine and Cormac's veins, and their joining had the potential to open the Emerald and Serpent Ways to them, old worlds only true Eadar can enter. But their love affair goes tragically amiss, with catastrophic consequences.

Etaine flees and as the years pass, slowly rebuilds her life, but the Fada's attacks grow more ferocious, and the Eadar are forced to fight for their very existence. When the Fada mass to commit yet more bloody slaughter, and the bands join in a final, desperate effort to defeat them, Etaine comes under Cormac's command, the very last Eadar she ever wants to see again.

Together they have a weapon that can destroy the Fada, but to use it, Etaine must learn to trust again and Cormac to Remember. And time runs short: the Serpent rises.

Heart Hunter – *a female hunter on an impossible quest*

Fleet is a young Sceadu hunter: skilled, strong, and fast. She hunts deep into the icy mountains, seeking meat for her people, for the rains have failed and plunged the Sceadu into hunger.

Her hunts are hard, but she has much to look forward to. Soon she will be gifted her air-name by the Sceadu's shaman, and then she will be a full adult, and free to marry the man she loves.

But while Fleet is on hunt, the old shaman dies, and the new shaman visions a very different future for her: cross the frozen, ice-locked mountains and complete a perilous quest or lose the man she loves forever.

In a moment of anger and frustration, Fleet commits a terrible wrong and sets out into the frigid mountains to atone with her life. In a journey that takes her deep into the earth's darkest places, into strange new worlds, and even into Death itself, she discovers that only she can save her people. To survive, she must draw on every shred of her hunter strength, and doing the impossible, it turns out, is just the beginning.

The Third Moon – *science fantasy with a very human quest*

Where does the past end and the future begin?

Haunted by inherited memories of his people's dispossession and theft of their children, Warrain is just twelve years old when the nightmare repeats. But Warrain isn't living on Earth in the 21st Century, he is living on the planet Imago in the far flung future.

Five years before, Station One's Mech's got high on the opioid arrash, and in the bloodshed that followed, Warrain's scientific community were expelled from the Station, his father murdered, and his mother and unborn sibling lost to him.

The scientists carve out a rudimentary Station high in Imago's ranges, and Warrain's friends get on with their lives. Not Warrain; he climbs the Tors to stare down at Station One, dream of his mother and sibling, and plot revenge.

And then one day, everything changes. A third moon appears in the sky, one of Imago's life-forms calls him by name, and disease breaks out at Station One.

When the Mechs visit to seek help for their ill, Warrain seizes the opportunity to deal them a blow they will never forget. But the third moon brings changes that threaten them all and, to aid the life-form whose kind is being dispossessed and slaughtered, he must turn his

back on the hate that has long sustained him and find
another way to live.

Messenger – *a dystopic future filled with hope*

In a world made deaf by hatred, who will hear the messenger?

Severine's world ends the day her family is murdered. Being raised in the loving community of gay Travelers always marked her as an outsider, but being female puts her in mortal danger. Women are scarce, precious, and hunted.

When chance brings Severine face to face with the father she has never known, he assigns the son of his murdered best friend to guard her. They soon clash. Severine believes all men are violent brutes and Jeph resents his freedoms being curtailed.

An uneasy understanding grows but Jeph is glad to deliver her to the Enclaves, a sanctuary her father has carved out in the mountains for his women and children. But there is no safety in a world broken by war and sickness and when violence follows her, Severine flees to the northern city of Andhaka in search of a home amongst her mother's people. Jeph follows, bound by loyalty to her father, but the north holds terrible dangers for him.

It's been years since Andhaka has welcomed outsiders with anything but bullets, and to survive and to protect Jeph, Severine must learn to use her enemies' weapons against them. As the stakes rise, she comes to understand the horror of her mother's loss, and what drove her father north seventeen years before. His quest becomes her quest, but she hasn't counted on the savage legacy that war and sickness have left behind, or on falling in love.

I Heard the Wolf Call My Name – *gender-fluid shifters in search of home*

Finalist Best YA Novel – 2019 Aurealis Awards

Jax is just twelve years old and in bird-form high above his island home, when it explodes, killing everyone on it. He believes he is the only survivor until ten years later, he comes face to face with his boyhood friend, Matiu.

Matiu is military and the military need shifters for a crucial mission, but Jax refuses. Having spent ten long years burying his bizarre shifter past, he isn't about to resurrect it. But Matiu rouses other feelings too that Jax finds harder to ignore.

As the military ramps up pressure to force Jax's cooperation, he shifts to bird-form and flees to the last remaining island where he crash lands in the middle of Anahera's vision-quest. She searches for her skin-spirit animal to transform her into a protector of her people, and dreams of finding the white-wolf, but finds Jax instead. To save him she must abandon her quest but her kindness only adds to Jax's turmoil.
To decide who he truly is and where he really belongs, he must first confront his painful past, but that isn't the worst of his problems. The forces that blew Jax's island out of existence now threaten Anahera's as well, and he might just be the only shifter who can save it.
And time is running out.

Fantasy Short Stories

The Gift – A Deep Fantasy Short Story #1 – free on my website at www.ksnikakis.com

Excerpt:

Thariel sat for a long time, surveying all around her, as if she ate the world that would soon be memory. Then she took the harness from the mare, and with soft words, thanked her and bade her farewell. Her own feet she turned towards the forest, tossing her face-plate aside as she went, so that her hair fell loose to her waist, then she discarded her chest-armour, the sword and dagger, her bow and quiver.

The trees closed in and she came at last to the lake Men call Menios and stood for a while on its shore. An owl cried and a mouse shrieked, and all around her the souls of the newly dead jostled in their journey to the void. She stepped into the water and the new life inside her quivered.

'Fear not, little one,' she whispered, in her own tongue. 'We are going home.'

The Tale of Prince Anura – A Deep Fantasy Short Story #2 – free on my website at www.ksnikakis.com

Excerpt:

I should have been happy, for she was beautiful. Dark rivers of curls, skin as white as moonlight on water, breasts softer than spawn, and she loved me well. But her chamber was small, no matter the comfort of her bed, and the old feelings of entrapment rose, as persistent as gas that bubbles from rot below still waters.

I sat at the casement and listened, as I had once loitered near the watery skin of the second world and waited. The moon grew large and small many times, but it came at last, as I knew it would. The soft lament on the night-time air, the song of a soul as confined as mine. It took me a journey of many days through the depths of a massive forest to find her tower.

Stone it was and sheer, and as remote as the third world's glimmer had once been. I sang to her and she answered with sweet melodies of her own and we made love as frogs do, with our voices. And when trust had built, she let down her shining ladder of golden hair.

Glass-Heart – A Deep Fantasy Short Story #3

Finalist Best YA Short Story, Aurealis Awards, 2019.

Excerpt:

Geth moved amongst his band, exchanging quiet words while they waited. Some he had fought with since the Tallon's foul ships had first found their shores while others had come later, when the burn of cot and kin had sent them from their valleys.

Hate drove them but hate was no shield against arrow and knife. It was fighting skills that kept them hale, and Geth ensured they had them aplenty. He needed them living, not just for their own sakes and his, but for what would come later. When the Tallon's stain had been scoured away, the destroyed must be rebuilt.

Kyth sat alone and he went to her and gazed about. 'The glass-heart's fled, has it?'

'I sent her to a place of safety. She will come to me when it is over.'

'Safety was what I wanted for you!'

'And what I wanted for Nyar.' Her eyes caught the star-sheen as she looked up at him. 'But you can't always have what you want, can you, Ceannasai?'

Dragon Sprite – A Deep Fantasy Short Story #4

Excerpt:

Genn rocketed straight upwards, not just because she enjoyed seeing the limitless blue sky before her, but because a Waiwin's wing shape made vertical flight harder for them. Orin didn't try to catch her but swept in circles around her, gaining height in an ever-narrowing spiral. It was a clever tactic and one Genn didn't believe hehad thought of in the instant she had cleared the trees. He had obviously studied her strategies and developed a plan to counter them *or so he thought*.

Genn waited until the spiral narrowed to *axeel*, the minimum distance a Waiwin must keep from a Velven unless she *accepted* him, then swerved towards him, narrowing the distance between them. Orin's eyes flashed to black, shocked she *had* accepted him, but before he could act, she folded her wings and dropped.

The strength that had driven Orin's pursuit had surged to his wing-tendrils in anticipation of locking them with hers and he would struggle even to stay airborne until it flowed back.